E·S·T·E·L·L·A

HER EXPECTATIONS

E·S·T·E·L·L·A

A Harvester Novel

THE HARVESTER PRESS LIMITED
Publisher: John Spiers
16 Ship Street, Brighton, Sussex

First published in 1982

British Library Cataloguing in Publication Data

Roe, Sue
Estella, her expectations.
I. Title
823'.914[F] PR6068.0/

ISBN 0-7108-0465-2

Photoset in 12 pt A.M. Deepdene by
Photobooks (Bristol) Limited
Printed and bound in Great Britain by
The Thetford Press Ltd,
Thetford, Norfolk

To Johnny

Part One

In a city, on a road lined with dusty trees, there is one house painted a faded blue-grey. On the window ledge, two feet. Feet that have known foreign streets and dancing. Bare floorboards and satin. Silk and the stage. Now sunning themselves in the city. As a backdrop to the feet, a tall, a sun-bleached, an aquiline woman. This woman has seen Paris, and theatre dressing rooms. She has been there, where Diaghilev redesigned the lines and textures of the body, and made it dynamic. This woman has known the taffeta and satin and grease-paint which puts dancing women on show. The dancing women. The women with colour. The painted women. But now she is old. She is to be seen, in the afternoons, taking the shade, slowly, along the dusty main road. She has a stick and she walks carefully, with grace, and very tall, in the dust and the silk of faded city leaves. Children visit her house, and are taught how to dance. There is a brass plaque on her gate post, giving her name. It says, Miss, and another word, which is faded. At concerts her child pupils dance. The concerts bustle with painted mothers and pastel etched children. Seated on benches, watching the spectacle. Tiny feet bound up in red satin. She is silent, the dancer, seated at the back of the room. She wears a sari. Silver and slender. Her grey hair is loose down her back. Kohl designs her eyes. Heavy brass and silver bangles adorn her long, slender arms. Jewellery from the East. The walking stick taps the ground.

This is the dancer, who lives in the blue-grey house.

In a city, on a road lined with dusty trees, there is one house faded blue-grey. Estella passes this house on her way home from the art school. Now it is summer time and she has nearly finished her training. There, near the end of it, in those hot, summer days, Estella walks past the blue-grey house and thinks that soon she will be an artist. But that first, she will enter a world unstreaked by paint. She will go out herself, into it, and be painted. She will be there; she will join in. Enter the designs of the world, explore between the lines of it, saturate herself in its colours. Inhabit the painted world. This is what she will do, thinks Estella in the dusty street where the hot sun paints pale city colours with a sheen of dust. In the autumn she will go to Paris and work in a gallery. It is all arranged. And, thus, on the brink of this arrangement, she can be her most free. Sometimes, as today, she walks past the grey-blue house, and she reads the name of a dancer on the gate post. The sound of a piano and the thump of light feet on floorboards is in the air. It comes through the window of the dancer's house where the dancer teaches dancing to children. Other days, Estella takes the bus home. From the top deck, she observes, sometimes, two feet, scarlet tipped, resting on the window ledge.

Estella sits at the long table, which seems to be made of floorboards, in the long, light room, and paints a crimson flower, to use up the end of some crimson paint and to complete a long day spent fitting small mathematical details onto canvas. The point of her flowers is to use colour to make them seem to be moving, by colouring them all unreal. So she paints a blue and crimson sunflower which seems to be bursting out of itself. The effect is achieved by the colour. No sunflower can bear that amount of crimson, and so the tapered petals thrust themselves up and outwards, as though to shake off these plush reds; to seek the light. No shade of yellow could show such verve, and so Estella paints them crimson, and lets them be dynamic. Such experiments, Estella likes making with her paint. She paints women, too, and she makes the same experiments. They pose in the pale milky pink and white of soft skin, and she paints them: all auburn and scarlet and magenta; their mouths and eyebrows too harsh; their smiles too sexually-explicit. She paints too much colour and thus too much movement in the lean forwards, the resting on folded, full arms, and thus they solicit and taunt, all hot and full with grease-paint. They master the canvas with a raunchy glamour, and the pale pink models, leaning over Estella's shoulder to see the pictures of themselves, smile and laugh and are pleased, to see themselves so vivid and so racy.

The colours of grease-paint, Estella uses, for her women and her flowers, and, so adorned, they lean and taunt and master their real, pale colours. Making masks, and painting them lurid, Estella paints wilting, decadent women, and fleurs fatales. Estella is the best in the school. She gets the prizes. But she wishes her own painted women, their arms full of crimson painted flowers, could go up onto the stage and collect the prizes. Because these, Estella thinks, represent the real Estella. Though the small, slim Estella, the blonde Estella dressed in black, with black-shadowed eyelids, is also the real Estella. But though people expect the blonde and black Estella to be the painter, they don't expect the painted women to be Estella.

Sitting at the floorboard table, in the room full of brushes and paints and sinks and bits of paper and metal and wood, in this room, putting small streaks and daubs to the flower picture, Estella decides what to do. This summer, until the end of the Autumn, when she goes to Paris, she will not paint any more. Instead she will take time out for herself. She will hang around in the world for a bit, like a yellow flower, just to see what's there. Some living, thinks Estella to herself, has to be done. The time has come. Making careful strokes of the brush, Estella reflects to herself on the possibilities: all the ways she will paint Estella.

This evening she walks home from the art school. A new flower is in her folder. She stops to buy a newspaper, and she crosses the road to the park. The green of it is shaded by city dust; the dust of lives and work, and it's for this shaded, muted colour that Estella loves the city. She likes the dank black-green of city privet-hedges. As though they've been brushed with news print. Like the thin, thin shadows of women's faces, travelling home on the bus at the end of the day: in the morning they had stroked and streaked and blended the peach and pink of apricots – but the news print has left its mark. It's hot in the early evening, and so Estella finds a bench, which looks as though it's made of floorboards, like her painting table, and spreads the paper over her lap, balancing it on the folder with the flower in. She turns to *Situations Vacant*, and the sun shines a yellow light, the light she leaves out of her flowers, onto the page. Domestic, domestic woman, woman, daily woman, au pair, holiday home, office cleaner . . . she reads. She thinks of the women who put the adverts in. They would have soft kid shoes, and hair furled and piled like meringue, and being women would be their whole lives. She's sure there's something about her, something biding its time, absent for the moment, held at bay, like the yellow lights she leaves out of her sunflowers – something in her own body, that makes her eligible to be one of these women. And indeed, when she gets to Paris she will be one if she isn't a painted woman, like her painted women. It will all be a matter of chance. There's hardly a dividing line between one kind of paint and another – the painted women it is, who get the chance to be one kind of visible woman or another – the hostess, the prima donna, the painted woman, or the painter. She's sure she's in with a chance. It's only the women who don't understand about paint who ruin their chances and never get noticed. The faded ones, who just do things for other people, and never invent their own things. If you wear plenty of paint people never try to take advantage of you. Estella's fingernails tip her fingers scarlet, and give her hands hard, strong edges. She turns the pages of the newspaper, and this time her eyes take in the names of the streets. And she notices one situation vacant, in the same street as the blue-grey house with the feet. The street just across from the park. She decides to go over, and look at the numbers. The house in the advert is the dancer's house. The dancer is advertising for a companion, to live in.

*   *   *

The dancer has put an advert in the newspaper, for a companion. Lodging and a small payment, for being there. The dancer is old and cannot take up all the space in the house, these days. She needs a girl, to take up one of the empty rooms. This will suit Estella. She paces the street, with the newspaper. Something about the peeling paint of the house, something about its decadence, definitely attracts Estella. She has spent the last few years of her still life learning to paint. She has learnt to make colour, and shading and lighting. Painted still lives and other women. A world of stark flowers and abstractions. And known how to make it live with a sliver of decadence. Studious in her dark blue overall Estella has concentrated for four years. Offered herself, submissively, to the mastery of her craft. And now, in the dancer's house, she can live in the world she has painted. In the dancer's house, Estella can be a painted woman. There on the streets in the harsh light of the early hours, all garish in grease-paint and stilettos. Here Estella will paint herself. Here she will have an alibi in the dancer; more dancer than woman, she too, will have painted the woman she is. Estella pushes open the gate, and knocks at the door, which is ajar. The dancer's voice calls her upstairs, to the room where the feet rest on the window ledge. Estella goes into the room and the dancer is leaning, one elbow resting on the keyboard of a grand piano, one ringed, large boned hand poised, as the door opens onto the dust; the parrot; the paintings; the dishes of chocolates. The dancing woman smooths her hair and her spine uncurls slightly; her posture fixes itself. The woman is upright and she faces Estella. My name is Estella, says Estella. I called about a room. The woman smiles, and so, she turns as she rises to offer Estella her ringed hand. And Estella thinks of all the years of thin, grey hair that must be furled into the elegant pleat at the back of the woman's head. The woman walks from the pelvis. From the bird's wing hip bones. Her long legs swing and stride grey flannel trousers, today. The woman's legs walk, again, for Estella, in Paris in the nineteenth century – causing stirs in drawing rooms. These are legs for salons. The woman raises dark eyebrows, slightly, at Estella. It's not a very grand room, she says.

She will show Estella and they go. They leave the colour, the parrot, the piano, the chocolates, the paintings. They open another door, together. The dancer directs Estella. She opens the door onto a sunny room. A light room, one entire wall a window. A spotted, framed mirror, propped upon a table. In the window a writing desk. On the longest wall a mantelpiece; above the mantelpiece a faded painting. Estella sees the painting. Framed, but with no protecting glass. Canvas exposed to the touch. The very texture of faded canvas, exposed, in this room. Over to the window walks Estella. Out of the window, the cascading amber of Autumn. Estella is there outside for a second in the lush, the amber impressionism. So many shrubs, so many large, red-leafed trees, so many roses, that the garden is blurred colour. Estella looks again into the room. She sees herself in the room, in the mirror. Tarnished and dusty, she is small and French, in a painting, in this room.

Who did the painting? asks Estella. On the mantelpiece a strange dark painting of a porcelain or marble statue. Estella looks closer. It's a porcelain Madonna. A goddess, turning proudly, or modestly, away. Swathed in Grecian white. And standing so close as to blur the perspective of the whole, Estella adjusts her eye to perceive, folded in the painted porcelain texture, a tiny white porcelain baby. Clinging to, climbing about, the torso of the white Madonna. Its legs trailing away into the folds of the body and dress of the mother; its right arm gesturing, bizarrely, away. Hardly there at all; a painter's afterthought. Only, one small fist clutching, or clenched, at the neck of the mother. Just under the chin. One small clenched fist holds the Madonna's gaze; focuses the

Madonna's pose. My mother. Replies the dancer. My mother was an artist. Put it in the cupboard if you decide to take the room. It's very old fashioned. Other people's choice of paintings can be irritating, in a room. She was at the Royal Academy, but she gave it up to have children. Estella moves over to the window. She looks out on a mellow Autumn of pears and shrubs; a leafy, auburn Autumn of apples and late roses. The Autumn, the auburn, of impressionism. Turning aside, Estella looks in the large, tarnished mirror and sees Estella. A figure in the room with the paintings. I'll take it, says Estella.

* * *

Estella moves in. Hones in on herself. Running up dusty roads to the train station Estella scuffs the leaves and trails her hand along the black basement railings of the houses. This is her road, now, and she claims it. She watches the people, walking in her road. The corner shop has its lights on: the bright hearth of the street. Faded women move up the hill carrying enormous bags of shopping. They had no choice. They feed their families, therefore they exist. It is right, to stand in the corner shop in a red dress and old shoes with stiletto heels at eleven in the morning, here. Here is the legitimate underworld. A world the functioning world never glimpses (it doesn't get out until five o'clock). Yet a world in which you are seen. Therefore, you exist. It's Sunday so today people mostly buy papers and cigarettes; sugar that ran out before the world outside closed down. And they are un-made up because just out of bed; or glossed and glamourised for the day. But tomorrow, on a real Monday in the luxurious, ambiguous world in which one can be in a shop at eleven in the morning; half dressed; in make-up just too garish for the half light of the domestic nether world: there will Estella dare just black eye-liner with no colour; a red dress with pink stockings; no coat on a cold and drizzly day. An element of risk, and theatre dressing rooms. Because there in the wings of the world for mothers and artists and old people and people with money; there you can be viewed without being accused. There in the world where there is no system and no transgression. No laziness because no deadline. No danger. And yet you are observed. Therefore you exist.

Feeling real, Estella takes a train and goes to collect her black suitcase. She packs her black clothes and her silk blouses. Her brightest make-up and her coloured stockings. Estella packs black lace underwear and Estella packs the ballet shoes she bought to feel her feet very flat on the floor boards; her spine unfurling; the backs of her heels stretching; her shoulders reaching. To feel the poise of sheer theatre in. Estella bought the ballet shoes. And so Estella packs the ballet shoes. Estella says goodbye to the pink room she lodged in while she went to the art school, with its nylon carpet and its miniature curtains; its suburban warmth. The warmth of true shelter. And Estella gets in her black leathery taxi, with coins for the tip loose and dirty in the pocket of her new silk skirt. Practising her new regime: letting beauty loose in the dirt. And takes her train back in to the dust. And goes back to the tree lined road, back to the peeling house. Her house, now. When Estella unlocks the door with the huge, heavy key, she smells wine and damsons and all the alcoholic heaviness of orchards late in the evening; hot in the late Summer. Estella puts her suitcase down onto the lino in the hall and looks down the corridor. At the dingy end of it, there where the light is just fading, where the corridor opens, without a door, onto the kitchen, the dancer stands poised as though at the bar. The dancer's spine is stretched easily and she stands very straight. And the dancer presides over her own hands. The hands stir damson juices; great casseroles of hot crimson. The hands move languidly somewhere above the bubbling and spilling crimson. They direct it, as the feet, resting on the ledge of the window, direct the sunlight. And the hair. The dancer's hair. The hair is loose and long; it reaches right to the base of the strong spine. And it's more completely grey than long hair on a living woman surely could ever be. A Victorian doll's hair. Estella wishes the dancer goodnight. She says, Goodnight, and, I think I will go to bed, to the dancer. The dancer says she supposes midnight is rather late to be making damson jam. And she sucks a large spoon, and tastes crimson.

Estella plays jazz. She turns on the radio and jazz is playing. It splinters in the night, and cracks the shadows. And downstairs in the half-light of the dim kitchen the dancer sucks crimson juices to the strains of a single saxophone while Estella lies down to sleep. Will she dream that the dancer, her hair frantically and treacherously down her back, the ladle damned with spots of crimson in one hand, will pace with poise outside Estella's room until, at a given moment, she slides her skeleton key in Estella's lock thus damning her to a life of solitude and exotic madness? No. She imagines such a scene to herself, to the strains of the back-street jazz; call-girls lined up amongst the dustbins. By the time the night is silent Estella is asleep. A dark, dreamless sleep. The pit of it.

In the morning the crimson has all slid into the dark and it's amber and orange again. Outside Estella's window there is a scarlet painted wooden chair under a tree. And a clay statue of three women. Life-like, posed on the grass in the auburn light. And the dancer strides the length of the lawn in a dress of pale grey-blue. She paces, in the early light. She picks up fallen apples. She walks towards the house. And when Estella opens her door, presently, onto the dank corridor of last night, she opens it instead on brightness and on the dancer, carrying small jars of brown chutney. In from a cupboard in the bathroom. The chutney is for Estella. Some food for her small cupboards. Estella wants to join in. And so she goes out to the front of the house and down the wide, the powdery steps. The dancer leans in the gateway, Estella thinks again of the call girls, and the grease-painted past of the dancer, backstage. The dancer is looking on, and smiling. There is something disarmed about, something taken away from the dancer. Estella tries to see where she is looking. At the front of the house, to the side of the powdery steps, at a secluded, a half-stated entrance to more steps leading down to the basement, is a magenta-haired woman. She is dressed in scarlet and she leans in the dancer's image. Her eyes are outlined like the eyes of the Egyptians: all in profile; but she is facing in Estella's direction. The woman is all henna and kohl, and Estella is a French schoolgirl beside her. The girl is in a doorway, on a film set. Tapered and garish. And making colours to live up to. Almost, soliciting. And yet she is too soft; too leaning and lilting, for her own magenta design. Estella goes closer, to see why. The dancer is introducing her. To her neighbours, who live in the basement, and look after each other, says the dancer. And, approaching, changing the perspective, Estella sees the clinging, the tumbling and tiny auburn haired baby. Nestling against taffeta and silk, and the dark painted colours, of the mother. Now Estella has a baby in the basement, as well as the chutney. She takes these things inside her mind. They signify: the chutney and the baby, and the magenta-haired woman. She touches the small, curled fingers of the baby, and the baby leans over to Estella. Mercy, says the dancer, this is Estella. And this is little Mercy, says the dancer, introducing the baby, the namesake of the mother. Estella furls the baby to her. In the sun the baby clings, roundly and darkly, to Estella, and the street gets a profile. Estella in black, and the little dark body clinging. The baby lends a subtle shading to Estella, and sets her profile in motion. Estella supports the baby. If the baby fell from Estella's side and dashed her head on the ground, she would die. The baby lives for a moment because Estella cares for her and draws the little body close. But the magenta Mercy is leaving to take the baby into the afternoon. Bye! says Mercy, waving the baby's hand. The dancer goes off into her house, and Estella goes back in, to sit at the window, and watch the view blur all auburn apricot amber.

In the dusty room the dancer, too, is going out into the afternoon. She takes her stick for a long walk and off she goes. Past the parrot, past the chocolate, and off into the city. She closes the door, behind her. A thin, ringed hand on the door handle. In the room, on a gold, fluted dish on the top of the piano, musty chocolates. If you bite into one you feel old, dusty chocolate go to powder in your teeth. You (Estella) bite into something hard, which shatters, softly. You know it is something hard by the taste (bitter), and the sudden soft brittleness. Poussière de menthe. In a chocolate. Chocolate gives, if you bite it, with a dull crack. Estella loves the sound of chocolate breaking. You bite down on it, thinking to end it, and it's still there in a layer of soft powder between your teeth. I would like to taste fabric, reflects Estella, biting the dancer's chocolate. I would have raspberry satin and caramel silk. I would have white velvet tasting of cream, and beige leather crème caramel. I would have a taffeta blackcurrent sorbet, and black velvet treacle; a soufflé of fine net and lace. I would go to the mud after a storm, and lick chocolate mousse. She has gone, the dancer. She goes to a café to drink lemon tea. She eats very little. She does not taste fabrics as Estella would like to. Her cheeks are hollow: there in the room with the musty chocolates; there in the cool, the pale café, smelling faintly of lemons. Dancers dance for their strength. Art for art. Dust to dust. Eating is for healthy children. Estella sits on the piano stool and leans her head against the keyboard. In the soft afternoon, she dreams in a light, half-sleep.

In France, in the country, there the health is rich and heady. Like alcohol. Estella bicycles in her dreams in the hot sun her brown fingers spread out into the air. Estella opens her fingers to the sun, there in France. Estella's head moves and the keys of the piano sound faintly. Making notes. The sun is entering between her fingers. It filters right through her fingers, and there is a space in the centre of her body which is opening and yielding, and Estella freewheels. Down she goes. Right into the sun. She wears a scarlet dress. Strawberries, vivid by the roadside. Her shoulders are smooth. The polished, brown knobs of walking sticks. Estella lifts the straps of the dress down over her shoulders and lowers it. She can make a V with her straight, her strong legs, and let the cycle take her into the sun. She would let the wind take her dress and fold it in its flourishing furls. It will not. It has no fingers. Winds do not disentangle. Winds cannot choose. There is no reason for the wind to take Estella's dress and hurl it away. It sighs, right through the strawberry fabric. When Estella is walking, or lying face down in the grass, she stoops, or stretches, to collect small, frail insects in her fingers. All colours. But nothing can fill the yawning which unfolds over Estella's whole body, the yawn which would keel backwards and cry out into the sun. Estella's skin is a nut skin. Her hair is sun-bleached blonde. In France, in the morning, after a hot night in a room with flaking shutters (she does not need sleep, with so much sun under her skin) she crosses a gravel path. Her footsteps crunch as in a movie. She enters the big house, and it is cool. The cool of stone; unlike the cool of the misty early morning outside. In the haze. The floor is stone; the room is cool. There is a geometric clarity, in this particular feeling; this being here. Estella pushes open the shutters. They heave out towards the morning. Flaking wood on splintering sunlight. She makes coffee in a bowl. She goes searching in the cool, stone kitchen for new bread and the confiture de maison. She brings them into the cool room with the window that looks out onto the morning. She puts the bread and the apricot jam and the warm bowl of milky coffee onto the hessian cloth, on the round table. She sits at the round table in her royal blue kimono. Her skin is gold against the blue. Her hair is twisted in a tail. She has cheekbones, here in the sun, made by swimming and cycling and stretching out to the sun on the hot grass. She sits, and stirs the coffee round and round, and the backdrop of sun gradually becomes more intense. She is Veruschka draped on a flaking wall in Greece. Sun-bleached and sun slimmed. She is a piece of excavated earthenware wrapped in a rag of silk; tanned; in her royal blue kimono. For preservation. And the Estella of her dreams is a leaning, wistful, a watchful and very beautiful French maman, preparing the bols de lait. She shows a concern for; la nourriture et la santé; la fortitude; la beauté; and she knows precisely what she envisages by each of these words. En face, de l'autre côté de la table, les deux petites filles la guettent des yeux gros, derrière leurs bols. Elles ont des cheveux bruns, épais, des yeux énormes. Elles président, elles sont aux aguets; elles ne questionnent rien. De bonnes choses; de belles choses, vont se passer devant elles. Little brown daughters, dressed in white broderie anglaise, little sleeves reaching to dimpled elbows. Little, tiny hands, that close over things, to keep them secret. You prise open a little fist and you find cream cheese. A little, treasured ball of it. Warming to the protective secrecy of the little palm. Little arms tip the big bowl of milk until the wide eyed face is lost behind it. Two little girls, with enormous, wide eyes. The little girls of Estella's dreams have eyes that know nothing. They don't know, there at the sunny table in the morning. All the details that need to be known for them to be women. French women, with all the details of majestic womanhood at their disposal, to be faced with grace, and with glamour. All the pretences and guises they will have, with dignity, to learn before it's time to curl and curl in the yards of luxurious white satin: the metamorphosis. To give themselves in marriage, to find themselves. Changed. Estella is seated (still dreaming) still and slim on the other side of the table. She will fold and hold them to her, and the little brown feet will curl and clutch. She is perfumed and pale. She will say, Venez, mes chéries, and they will run out into the fields. She is dressed in a dress by Yves Saint Laurent of crêpe de chine. She is unruffled, just caressed by the breezes, and can look this way whether she writes letters at a desk or paints at her easel or goes out into the hot sun to buy chocolate and bread for goûter. She is, unnecessarily beautiful. She does not need to be so beautiful. She has designed her good looks for this picture. She is a beautiful and amoureuse French maman. Et où est mon mari? Il est au bureau. Il rentre pour le déjeuner. Il rentre pour le dîner. Il m'adore. He is crisp in iced white and bitter black. Who are you? asks Estella. He is sleek and brittle. He does not have the softer, the stronger shape of the little girls, who will be there in the world for ever. Le mari might just walk off the set at any moment. But when the light has gone Estella will go to her bed, perfumed and creamed, with a change of (more delicate) jewellery, and after she has kissed the little girls and caressed them to sleep, she will go to her tender lover, who will make her soft like the little girls. But the lover, in the dream, has a face without outlines. Is he the French papa? The dream screen is blurred. The brittle French papa drives out into the night, out beyond the credits. His footsteps crunch on the gravel in black patent shoes. He wears bitter, brittle black, and sparkling white. Plain chocolates and iced martini. He opens the door of the silver Alfa Romeo. He slides in. A sliver of lemon. He shuts the door. Canapés. Schnaps. Estella and the lover stand together, leaning over the cots of the little girls. They are the little gorgeous ones. They preceded the lover. But the lover has been there for always. He will be there for always. The brittle papa is seared and struck by splintering glass. There he is in the dressing room, pulling off the black patent shoes. Flinging the black dinner jacket over a chair. He sits upright and precise at the tarnished mirror. Before the bare bulb, in the searing light, he takes off the make up. Perhaps women spill in with flowers and kisses. But whatever happened to the soft lover with the real, large, tender face. The one who had special words for the little girls and who caressed Estella into existence. There is a filtered light. Or an over-exposure. Slow motion. A blurred perspective. When the shot of the French countryside settles and resolves; when you see the still, just before the final credits; when the music stops, the picture is out of focus. Impressionism, in close up. You are forced to stand back. Even Estella, who loves art above all else, for whom the painting precedes the reality (if that is not to give too much away), is forced to stand back. Away from it.

In the evening, in France, the light is dimming. It has been hot. Baking, blazing, hot. And now the air from outside is cooler. The light is bright inside. They sit around the table. Five pairs of bronzed, boned, ringed hands. Estella is the jeune fille; la petite; la mignonne, now. The other pairs of ringed hands are older than Estella's. The rings are brassier; the skin less gold leaf. They flip the cards, face up, on the table. Flip flip flip slap. And they curl their cool hands over tiny insects. They crush the fine bones of the insects with the brittle tips of their fingers. They delicately crush. They toughly crush. The insects are coloured as with brush tips. Fragile and frenetic. Humming, and swooping, and fluttering. In the pool of light which the cards dip towards, insect after delicate insect. Shatters. They crush them and they suck toffees from a box. They wring them in their fingers. They push the table, on a particular spot, with one scarlet-tipped finger, and they take the finger away. They leave a small black mark behind, where the insect was. They have eaten: poulet au pot; ratatouille; lapin aux prunes. Or just a large, bloody, flaming steak. Straight up, with a frazzle of garlic.

They have drunk red wine. They have sucked purple plums, or chocolate mousse. Black in the dusk. Now they suck toffee. And their ringed, boned hands, tingling from the sun, sift the cards, and crush the insects. The French women: the women at play.

* * *

Estella wakes to the feel of an insect, crushed somewhere under her skin. The keys of the piano are hard, beneath her head, and in the late afternoon the dancer's faded room casts shadows over itself. The tapestries and the old chocolates and the faded curtains of the dancer's room settle themselves on a thin ledge inside Estella. This is the dancer's room, and she has dreamed of France at the keyboard of the dancer's piano. And if the lights are dimming the afternoon must be drawing in. The dancer will soon be back and so Estella must go to her own room again. She leaves the dancer's room and crosses the corridor to her room, the bright room where the window looks out on the auburn Autumn. But the colours are deepening. Estella goes to the window, and sits in the window seat. Now that she is here in the dancer's house, she thinks again about the things she ought to settle, now that she can be a painted woman, and not a painter any more. At her window there is a red curtain which drapes the length of the window, down to the floor. Estella pulls the curtain against the dark outside.

* * *

Mercy, in the basement, pulls the curtain, and wonders what's wrong. The curtain is heavy, faded green. The room is untidy and the baby's things are strewn, on the backs of chairs and on the floor. The room is always rather dark, because it is below ground. Mercy leans in a forward-upwards-and-out movement, to look out of the window. The view, at this up-and-out angle, is a dingy privet hedge. A full, dull curtain, something grown and then arrested, between Mercy and the outside. Inside the room Mercy has a bottle of wine on the table, with her make-up. She drinks the wine. This helps. Yet something is wrong. Mercy feels the wrong like a small, heavy greyness in the pit of her stomach. Low down and aching, a wrench. A dull one, like washing being wrung. Inside Mercy, the small dull knot of greyness. Outside Mercy, the privet hedge. It is what is between them that's wrong, she realises, as she pulls the curtain. What is between them is the gypsy.

* * *

Estella pulls the curtain against the dark outside. Now that the light has faded and the curtain and the dark shut out the amber Autumn, Estella's room casts shadows, like the shadows in the dancer's room. The light in the dancer's house is not very good. Now that there are no lights of apricot and amber, reflected in the room, the room becomes a city room. There in the shadows, there in the darkness. It's a room for wearing taffeta in. Estella will get some. Taffeta that crackles, and black stockings, and red silk scarves. She will get all these fabrics, to wear in the room when the curtain is pulled against the darkness, and she will look in the small spotted mirror propped on top of the small cupboard, and she will see a spider-lady Estella, all thin strands of black, threaded with red. All tight in taffeta, a new picture of Estella to fit between the blonde Estella dressed in black, and her own painted women. The spider lady of the tarnished mirror, Estella will be. And, thinking of spiders, Estella remembers the gypsy she knew long ago, when she first went to the art school.

Estella had loved a gypsy. She loved him from afar, even after she had got to know him. She loved the gypsy, and paintings. And had decided long ago that when she fell in love she would love as an artist loves. She would travel, and she would paint, and she would love a gypsy. She would sit on the steps of a gypsy caravan wearing a wide, scarlet skirt all gold embroidered. Her earrings would show, because her black hair would be swept back off her face and fall down her back, thickly. She would sit on the steps of the gypsy caravan with her legs wide and her blouse cut low, and in her lap would be a small gypsy baby, with very black hair and its own small earrings. Like the Indian babies. This is how the gypsy fitted in. He would be there in the background. He would gallop away on the horse, roughly embracing her in his haste; he would hurry back, loaded with exotic fabrics for her to sell. She would sell them by sitting on her step nursing her baby: rich people would draw up in their cars and buy them. And she would observe the pretty women in pale pinks and diamonds, their blonde hair in folds sprinkled with diamonds. And not regret her choice – to be the gypsy's wife.

And so, when she noticed the gypsy who read a newspaper in the red flocked pub she went into, she knew that this was her gypsy. He wore a shirt of small checks, which was a good choice for reading a newspaper in, she felt. His shoes were polished, and gleamed like patent. And she couldn't decide whether he was reading the newspaper, or waiting behind it for someone to arrive. He seemed to have serious business there, where most people went to play. She passed close by him. It was Le Figaro. It was upside down. The gypsy raised one eyebrow behind it. His other eye stared. Estella went to the pub, to see the gypsy. She sat in a red flocked corner, on a seat with a slit, slashed by a knife. The stuffing was leaking out, gently. She sat in the half light and waited for the gypsy. She looked down, meanwhile, at her crossed knees, cadaverous in black stockings, in the shadow of dusk and gloom, and she observed the bones of her knees. She thought she had knees like a Jean Rhys heroine.

In the red plush of the mock Victoriana, where the magenta seats made shadows in the gloom and offered a respite from the outside for tired and sunken eyes, here, smoke clinging to the plush, to the faint smell of hashish, Estella pushed among the people, balancing her martini. She threaded the air, and its smokiness clung to her thinly. In all the corners of this room the people seemed to be waiting. Everyone was thin, in those days, and that mattered. People dyed their black hair blacker and starved their thin bodies thinner. Girls wore high leather boots over their knees. Their faces were shaded with shadows and lines of sleeplessness, and shadows and lines of paint. Some girls could take such shadows, such lines, right outside onto the pavements. Pushing battered prams through grey and milky-lit streets, past houses where green milk bottles lay upturned on grey grass. Black girls sunned themselves darker, dressed in bright colours for it. They leant against the walls. They sprawled on steps. Men in denim with muscles in their arms leapt over broken walls with one arm to steady them, wearing one earring, or two. People had a being, out there in the sunshine and the debris. Estella wanted to be there too. So she walked through the district, rather fast, and watched them all. She knew they didn't realise how much a part of them she felt herself to be. Though she had no place there. But this was where the gypsy lived, she knew. Out of this debris of derelict houses and no money, he came. He banged one of these front doors behind him and ran to the pub with his newspaper, she knew. A woman in a red dress sat on one of the steps nursing a baby, and waited for him to come back with the haul. This was why Estella walked in this district. She wanted to get to know it. And think about being there, with the gypsy.

The walls of the pub were the borders of a secret. The atmosphere got in your eyes. People cut spaces through it: squeezed past and pushed one another silently. In the corners, the smoke clung and stuck. A small, slight man with very black hair threaded and slid. A slight, dark man with a shirt of small checks, and a newspaper: he pulled it out of his pocket. One blue eye, one pale blue glass eye. When he moved he made a tangible absence, behind him. A door swung. He was there. A door swung. He was gone. In a shadow, raising one small booted foot from the ground behind him, he hooked twists of silver in a single finger. He was at someone's back. The person's fingers curled around the silver paper. On the pavement, in the banana-yellow light of outside, quickly, quickly, he ran, threading in and out of parked cars. He carried the newspaper, rolled. As he ran, he flicked the occasional lamp post with the paper. To get up speed. Estella watched the whole transaction, enthralled. She watched from inside until the door swung and he was gone. Then she ran outside and watched him in the distance, skating in and out, through the cars. Then she went back inside, and watched the woman who had taken the silver twist of paper.

Coming in through the mahogany revolving door, walking tall and thin, bringing in black from the darkness outside, Estella, observing, watches the woman and is not seen by her. She leans on the bar. You have never seen legs lean that way. They are bright scarlet stockinged legs. Backless shoes. So the legs go on and on and the back of the heel is pure scarlet. The back of the heel, so soft in babies. Her grey and scarlet dress, her bright royal blue dress, her silver lurex dress, reach to just above the backs of her scarlet knees, and her hair is magenta henna. The bar is mahogany; stained. The bar made, you suppose, a slightly concave angle with the scarlet legs. You have never seen a shape such as those legs made. Yielding to the concave; scarlet and yielding. Leaning legs. She had the proudest face you have ever seen. A model's face. Or a tiger's face. She had the proudest walk you have ever seen. Her scarlet legs, her proud, poised body, asserted independence. And cool contemplation. One part of the body or the other. She was fire in the grey smoke; auburn taffeta on grey silk. I am that woman. Says Estella. I am auburn; maroon; scarlet on grey. And so, in the lighting of a nightclub, or, in the lifting aside of a silk skirt, Estella can find herself, from now on and for ever and ever, in such a flame. Estella sees a self in the vividness of such an other as the woman. Looking down, seeing a thin, crossed knee, a thin ringed hand, Estella is a black spider. An insect born of pen and ink. Ringed and crawling; knuckled and brittle. But prouder and with more witchery than all the firebirds in Arabia.

Seated at the curtain in the dark room in the dancer's house, remembering the gypsy, remembering the woman, seeing in her mind's eye, the gypsy, the woman, the spider-woman in the tarnished mirror who will be Estella, Estella casts her mind into the spaces between them: the gypsy, Estella, and the auburn, flaming, scarlet woman with legs that lean. And sees: Mercy, in the basement, is the scarlet woman.

A kind of edge, then, sets itself up between the floorboards.

Part Two

Spiders have two possibilities for legs. They have slender fingers, knuckled and boned. And they have threads, like the frayed ends of black cotton left behind after the sewing is done. They are little black pits of ink and mystery, fringed with reaching, stroking fingers. Trailing wisps of telephone wire. Feathered, finely. Bewitching insects, spiders, they can touch and brush and reach. For that people fear them. They fear the black pit, right at the centre of the spider. Ink. That pit kills, in some countries (in Arabia?) Spiders have network fingers. Tube-line fingers. Estella watches a spider, threading itself into the dust, on the floor of the dim bar. Mercy and Estella drink red wine in smoky bars at midday, today, and they drink to their solitude. Mercy wears magenta. Estella likes black, spidery and shady. And so, they cross the pavements, avoid the traffic, and sit in bars, together. Once in a while, when they can arrange it, as today. They drink and drink. To make a little dazzle, a little sparkle. They lean and tumble and slide, a little. They eat gateaux and chocolate. To substantiate themselves. To know they are there. To make a heaviness. As, they paint their faces. It's vivid, when Mercy and Estella go and paint the town; see the city in new, dark colours. Down they go, into the underground. They say things to remember, there in the dirt, in the tubes. Going to meet Mercy, Estella cried. She wore her favourite black spidery trousers for the underworld, and read, on the train, a magazine featuring designs for kitchens and children's clothes. Ads. for cut price groceries, and recipes. Problem pages. There must be a lot of women who are eligible for these details: they fill many, many magazines. Estella reads an article. A woman has a miscarriage. Not a precise one. Not, a clinical one, all over very soon, under a bright light. Not, simply, an absence. But a whole labour, all in pieces. Clots and rags and tatters of a baby. The blood scarlet and heavy for several days. Not letting you turn the other way. If you put even a small spider in a box and open the box, men turn away. Estella's tried it. Men hate spiders because they don't know why. Estella had cried for the pieces of the baby, on the train, and cried, at the same time, for solitude, and for a strange, sad anxiety, somewhere deep in the pit of her. Estella reaches out for something. Into the black. And then, at the station, Estella and Mercy hug each other. Mercy is scarlet and magenta. The colour she puts into the air makes things better. In the dust of the dirty city, Estella says, I will always love men who leave me, Mercy. Every time, I always stay knowing what will happen in the end, and then I watch them leave me. I observe the whole process. I say, the worst thing he can do is kill me with the misery, and then I'm dead and in a box and I won't know about it. They were on an escalator at the time. Mercy said, sliding down behind her past the adverts, I think the worst they can do is not kill you, isn't it. I think you like the fear of death in them. Estella turns round to face her. She's now sliding down back to front. Her eyebrows gesture a silence, for Mercy to register. So, Estella and Mercy pass their day. It's time to paint the town again, time to smile. Estella gives Mercy a birthday card, on the steps of the National Gallery. It is cold and grey; already September. On the card is an enormous glossy picture of the inside of a cherry cup chocolate. You feel inside it, looking at it. Just from observing it, you feel you're in there. It oozes. Mercy and Estella are cold and grey as the day. Estella feels her hair is losing its colour, that day. She says, have a delectable birthday, and she smiles. They drink and drink, that day. They drink everything into place. They tell all the pain of things and the shadows of things in brittle words, in plush bars. They just, recount everything. All the pieces. The wine in her head, Estella tells Mercy about the lover who preceded the gypsy. The door was closed. He had gone. She tells her the throbbing in her body, the waves of panic. The shock of cold sweeping over her whole body. A scream, growing over her body, and out of the pit of her. She tells Mercy the wrench of it. Some of it. One, now dead, fragment of it. A whole dead piece of it. Mercy knows. She knows it. And so they sit, and drink, and walk in the dirty streets together. A workman whistles down at them from his rooftop. Sitting together, leaning all over each other in the dank, the grey, the hollow and echoing underground lines. They sit inside those lines most of the day, going here and there, and, all through the city, men in jeans stare at them and call over to them. City gents' eyes twinkle. Gangs of boys are beside themselves: the notion that Mercy and Estella, by turning their heads the other way and walking on, act as the silent, unobserving audience, is hilariously exciting. And Estella and Mercy want to be themselves, by themselves, and spend their day, not counting the interruptions and disturbances of this kind, doing just that.

* * *

At the weekend Estella gets away out into the world again. The dancer's house is too solemn for a Saturday. Dashing in glamorous black at Victoria, adjusting a black lapel, fastening the flap of her black leather bag, organising a ringed hand into a gesture to expose the ring, she's welcomed. There is one man who sees in Estella a woman of sophistication. He sees a Garbo face, the face of a woman who wants to be left alone – on show – constructed as it is, in his eyes, in the features of a design that stands apart from the ordinary mould. He wears, accordingly, a black suit with a grey silk tie, and, seeing Estella alone in the crowd, watching her stroke her eyebrows into their line, in preparation, he dashes to Estella and holds her close. This is not affection. This is approbation. Estella is alone again and starting once more to make the tasteful shapes of solitude about her dress. Estella has been loved. And he hated the chaos of her, then. Now she's re-surfacing – coming back up into the real world, the world of light and fashion: the surfaces of art. And it's a kind of homecoming. He says, Guess what, Andy's found a new girl: oh, so attractive. But not as attractive as you, my darling. And he means it, again. Andy is his boyfriend, but he has been concerned for Estella. She matters. Estella went to Paris, this summer, he has heard. She could have gone to the Moulin Rouge. She could have kissed a Frenchman in the Luxembourg Gardens, a millionaire in the Place de l'Opéra, made love in Montmartre. Eaten in a small, cool white restaurant over the bridge from Notre Dame, and had lavished on her a whole trousseau of silk dresses from Yves Saint Laurent. But, oh, relief. He has learnt about Estella's trip of solitude. Estella went alone. She sat in Parisian cinemas every afternoon. She watched *Madame Claude* and *Last Tango in Paris* and she cried in the dark. In the hollowness of old lift shafts; ignored by the exquisite brittleness of French women, lingering in the doorways of the sombre Notre Dame, avoiding the stumps of the beggars, looking out from the small balcony of her apartment, in the cooling air of dusk, towards the shining Sacré Coeur: Estella breathed the French air of gauloises and perfume, alone. The Champs Elysées shines at night and there is the sex of money in the air there. You have to walk in a dream, your stilettos just scratching the surface of the pavement. You can't avoid the erotica of Paris: the light at night is so indigo. It filters Paris so profoundly that the pavement is hardly there under your feet. Only the light is everywhere. But Estella, in the special light, skimmed the surfaces alone. She looked on and she was looked on. Trapped between looks, she was unable to take part. The man, too, knows all this now, and so he can smile and be proud again, for now again he can have Estella at his side. Walking apart. Thinking her own thoughts. Enjoying her detachment, and his. And their mutual enjoyment of it. Estella, his glossy magazine model. His accessory. The camp attention to detail, which women share. He wears her, as he sometimes wears his carnation or his ivory cane. And he is proud because he assumes the whole world is looking on, and giving him credit. Because he found her. He chose her. And so again he can stop worrying about the Estella outside his vision. The blurring, the unsettling effects on his image of nights and rooms in which men caress Estella and re-mould her and give her a slightly strained, a detached alertness. Which lends an unfamiliar liquidity to her eyes. He admires Estella's new steely jet earrings from Paris. He likes her neutral in black, because then he can see her as he likes. Marilyn Monroe; a modern dancer at the bar in a picture book. A sad lady at a window who cries. An artist's model. There is no shadow at Estella's side now to haunt him and hurt him with its opacity. He likes there to be nothing to penetrate. Then he has triumphed, because she's all his. Estella has been cleansed and forgiven in Paris by her loneliness, and so now, here in the city, she is a mannequin at his side. No-one can touch her because she is at his side for a few hours. She walks in his private world, beside him. A secret, but a clearly defined world. Estella is no longer lost to the tenebrous underworld. And so, for him, the people dazzle again, and Estella catches something of the dazzle, and of the off-beat glamour of two chiselled worlds in calculated collaboration. One sort of comfort; one sort of proxy.

They walk in step and he motions people aside and sweeps Estella into the space. It is his view that Estella should have an elaborate space around her, and he creates it for his credit. What can Estella do, under the mask of her quiet perusal of all this, but play the role; oblige him? She tells him what she's been dreaming to herself. And, there in the subway, a real face in the row; a real black petal, she's no longer the lonely woman in the garret: left behind, by the crowd (somewhere) downstairs. Here she sits in the real crowd. Going somewhere. There with a purpose. She tells him how she sits upstairs in the dancer's house, to the sounds of the little auburn baby, and how its mother is magenta and scarlet. A baby's mother has a purpose. Other women, the black and white, the tinselled ones, are undermined at her side. Estella is well prepared. She plays the piano speaks French she can embroider she dances she paints. Estella knows how to dress she knows how to charm she knows how to sympathise. He envies Estella. He wants to be her. Estella envies the goddess he adores; the self he has her create, in her own image. And she wishes she could actually be there.

*　　　*　　　*

Estella and the man, Clive, go to his magenta flat. Up the black steel lift the clashing gates and the bottomless drop, and into the flocked magenta. There are low little black tables and high Corinthian pillars balancing busts. There is a stuffed bear in the hallway and a tall stand for umbrellas with bird's head handles. There is a real public bar from the Nineties, all glittering with bottles and mirrors, and it makes a Renoir painting of the hallway. There are Victorian dolls on the chairs, and tassels and feathers and tapestries reflected in mirrors which are all around you. Where do the mirrors begin? Where does the room end? Which is here in the room and which is in the mirror? Which is Estella's reflection; which is Estella? In the room you don't know where you are. The delineations are ambiguous. And so you, Estella, are muffled, and closeted, and protected, in this room, spread with glossy magazines, open at the pages where all the boyfriends pose to model fashion.

Today Andy's new girl is coming to model, and Clive's apartment seems to bristle; to be sharpening its nails and its knives, making ready for the imminent intrusion. It's Clive, not the room, though, who makes the atoms prickle.

*　　　*　　　*

Clive is a commercial artist, and his flat is an artist's flat. He designs book jackets and soup can labels and bigger jobs: ads for cars and girls. And so, at one remove from the magenta flock; two from the lift shaft, there is a studio. The studio's a surprise because it has its own lighting. There is a very large window and the light shines white through it. The room is tomato soup coloured. This is the only room in the apartment where lighting is to help you see more clearly. There are no mirrors and no flocked magenta wallpapers, no tassels or velvet. Here the walls are painted plain translucent tomato soup, and the room is almost entirely taken up by an enormous table. There are borders round it just big enough to walk or sit in. The table is split into sections; there are different kinds of work on different parts of the table. The white light that comes in the window is picked up by overhead spotlights. So everything is clearly defined and you see it for what it is – here the lighting is put on, like your glasses. In the other rooms, lighting makes shadows and shadings and recesses, in the room, and masters the style of it: there, the lighting is applied like make-up.

Estella is taken into the studio to see the new work. Diagrams in the stark colours of children's crayons are stuck onto bits of card, and pieces of tracing paper are stuck over them. The bits of card for the adverts of cars and girls are large, the ones for the book jackets are small. Clive shows it all to Estella. Keeping her in touch; his eyes elsewhere. It would be nice to go to the French restaurant. He's been stuck indoors all day, crayoning the bits of card and sticking tracing paper over them. He craves the street and the night sky. He's done too many to feel delighted when one's finished. It would be *nice*, he says, to have a studio: to go out to work,: down the lift shaft, through the city streets, into the underground, up, into the daylight. A tall city building with several plaques on the black front door: up the chalky steps, and into the office. Instead of being there already. Like Mercy, says Estella, stuck behind the privet hedge, the commuters filing behind it: up the hill, into the station. A Gershwin tune starts up loudly from the hall. This is the doorbell.

Mercy is here, without the baby Mercy. She's come to see

Andy, who wants to take her photograph. Put her in print.

On the other side of the corridor, is the boyfriend Andy's studio. Andy gleams. He's the light, white, tomato soup side of Clive and Andy, Clive is the dark, the magenta flock. Andy appears in the pages of *Vogue*: posing for images of himself, to balance out the woman, to give them a focus. And perhaps even sell a few tweed suits, some leather jackets. This is his real work: to be photographed. But he also likes to take photographs of women. This is how he got started: he was photographing a woman from the media, and she took him to a party. There, he was seen. Being photographed, he makes a living. But taking photographs, he is master of the genre. This is why he likes it. He takes his shots of women all poised and unattainable, all shaded apricot and dressed in designer clothes. He sets grace, ease, and control in their faces, in the dark-room. They all look like Princess Michael of Kent. Estella smiles to herself to think of Andy in the dark-room, creating a whole series of Princess Michaels: making women and princesses of himself. The image of Andy rugged in tweed in the pages of *Vogue* complicates the notion somehow, but Estella can't quite think how. They are here in the studio: Estella, and Andy, and Mercy, looking at the photos of smiling, graceful women. The ones who manage to look like nymphs even in their clouds of maternity muslin. They all preside: Andy's peaches and cream. Andy shows them all off: every one. They stroll, they survey, they contemplate: images of apricot women.

* * *

Waiting in the magenta room for Mercy, made beautiful by the camera, to emerge, from the studio where Andy makes soft lines of her face and body, and will print them in pastel shades, waiting for Mercy, they sit, Clive and Estella, and they preside over pâté and red mottled cheeses and salami arranged like sliding dominoes. A bottle of champagne shows off the new champagne glasses. Wide glistening bowls on thread-slim stems. Pieces from inside a buttercup, slid out of the yellow and left in the dew to expand and glow, and lose their colour to the dew. And Andy's sister rushes in out of storms, or traffic, her hair frizzed for an advertisement for *Country Life* fabrics and Estella goes to look for Mercy. Mercy has finished the photographs and sits on the steps of the studio French window. Her back to the white walls, the parquet floor, the cameras, the large slices of print, the big blue cushion, the high white table. Mercy sits with her back to the space, taking up, now, none at all. The room is spacious behind her. Mercy, sitting on the edge of it, teetering on the brink of it, almost nowhere.

Estella goes into the space and sits softly down on the steps with Mercy. Mercy looks at Estella, half concentrating. Abstract. She smiles a little, abstracted. Distracted. Expressionist. Back into the Sixties, the spaced right out Sixties. Just for a long, a lingering, moment. Mercy says, Andy wanted me to be of my time. There's a photo of me somewhere thin and dressed in black and walking down a thin path in, somehow, black countryside. My hair is blonde and my cheeks are sunken and the picture says nothing. That was the Sixties, when you just photographed or painted and said nothing. You just showed it in straight lines. I suppose the Seventies glamourised all that, says Mercy, lingering. Mercy's legs are two thin lines, tapered. One bent at the knee to make two geometric angles. Seventies art brought colour. It brought a kind of explicit climax, it burst the borders where the Sixties had walked the tightrope of the black and white edges. Girls were thin and looked like diagrams, says Mercy. This worries her. The Sixties was Imagism in lines, she says, Superimposed lines, black on white. In the Seventies, the colour came in. All dark burgundy and magenta. Did you notice those colours? Mercy asks Estella. Estella nods and smiles. She's thinking that Mercy herself brought them back, when she leaned in magenta and scarlet, in among the mock Victoriana. All the record sleeves changed, says Mercy. A whole new world of space-age porn. And everybody got sombre and spaced out. It depends where you were, doesn't it, says Estella. But you knew *who* you were, says Mercy, because you noticed the changes happening. What changes are there now? How do you situate yourselves in time? Punk. Says Estella. That's a denial of change, says Mercy, in an old voice. I liked it in the Sixties, when you knew what shape you were supposed to be. You liked it then because you were in your prime, says Estella. Mercy smiles. There's no future in old designs, says Estella. She says it to Mercy. But Mercy's far away in an empty space. They sit side by side on the edge of the studio, on the steps, the two of them, a blonde little clear-thinking one, and a magenta of the shadows.

Andy comes to get them for lunch and champagne. And there they linger, the four of them in Clive's regal dining room, and they break off piece after piece of red-dappled cheese; they lift little circles of salami; they dip with their knives into taramasalata, and they sip the champagne until everything on the table merges, the colours are blurred and smeared, and the light is too dazzling.

Onto this light and this champagne, the door should open. The gypsy should come. Flick the doorbell with his rolled up newspaper, up the lift shaft, and into the flocked magenta. His one eye would splinter the light of the Moet et Chandon, his shoes would gleam. He should come now, when Estella's body fizzles to the light and the champagne, and the others are too sleepy to notice. He does not come.

* * *

Andy dashes away all in leather to his next job. Clive is asleep among the magenta cushions. There is so much champagne inside and outside Estella: in her breasts, outlining her sides like thin pencil marks, that she can hardly breathe. Oh, Mercy, she says. What shall we do? What shall we ever do? She sits careless on the apartment floor, her air is soft and pale blonde, its colour lifted by the magenta, and the Moet et Chandon. Mercy wants to see her photograph, but Andy didn't have time to develop it today. Let's go out on the town, says Mercy. We could buy wasp-waisted corsets dripping with ribbons, all vulgar and haughty. She lifts her nose, carefully, and so controlled, as though she balanced something precious on the end of it. And shiny green suspender belts. We could drape them over our arms and bring them back to show Clive. What larks! They laugh. Ssshh! whispers Estella – she puts her index finger, straight, up before her lips. Clive is asleep. They giggle at him. Though they like him really. But they have drunk so much champagne that they laugh a lot. You laugh with your whole body, says Mercy to Estella. Do I? says Estella. *Do* I? She laughs with her whole body at Mercy: at her humour; at her auburn, amber glow. I should paint you, Mercy, she says. I should redeem you from the line of princesses. You have an amber colour which Andy will get wrong. Mercy raises her eyebrows, shrugs her shoulders, slants her cats' eyes: Why not? she says. Why not? says Estella.

* * *

In the white tomato soup studio they find a small space. Estella sits at the table to paint. Mercy sits on the other side of the table. She leans on her arms, she is framed by the window and its white light. Into the afternoon, Estella paints Mercy. She finds a small piece of the art work card, and on it she paints the strong lines and the amber colours of Mercy. Mercy leans on her folded arms and smiles the champagne. Her mouth is amber, her eyes are bright in the white light from the window. The champagne has made each of these features autonomous. The eyes shine; the mouth curves: autonomous, each separate. Estella paints Mercy in streaks and curves. There is champagne in her paint brush. She daubs curves of amber arms and full, amber breasts in a kind of swelled pointillisme. She paints Mercy the burnt lights of the late Autumn afternoon; or a late Summer evening. A brightness, now fading. The auburn after-glow of them. She paints her mouth the same, strong auburn.

The arms of Mercy lean, in Estella's painting, on a strong edge of indigo shadow – where, in real life, the table would be. Then she paints her strong, straight eyebrows. She paints these black. The black, she gives her, as homage to the gypsy – as though he might have left his mark in Mercy's face. As, indeed, he must have. She gives her shadows and points of black hair, too, like the gypsy's. She smooths the shadows and outlines of the face a smoke-black, showing, in the face, the city. And then she paints the views through the dancer's windows in: she daubs a harlequin background of green and yellow and auburn leaves. The yellow and auburn of the leaves she sees through her own window; the green of Mercy's privet hedge. The grey, the charcoal, the coal-dust green. Dusted black. The result is – Estella stands back a little – a bland and brash and clownish yellow, all daubed with auburn and green. The yellow seems to predominate, which is strangely not what Estella had intended. Not like the view through the dancer's window at all. More like the stage curtain for a pantomime. So much yellow: the effect is oddly sunny. This must be because the white light of the window: the present, filtered in. And so to counteract it Estella daubs stronger lines of auburn for the cheekbones, and since there is still too much yellow, she paints a weird halo of auburn roses. This she paints in swirls and circles. She adds streaks of soft ivory, which might be feathers in a strange, amber hat. Or might be the white lighting, filtering through even this last absurd gesture.

The woman in the painting leans and narrows her eyes and the whole vivid ensemble of black and auburn, the colours of the painted woman, seem somehow to draw the eye to the curve of her arms: as though the whole mass of the painting were rested there. Leaning and curling, and supporting the body of the woman. Somehow separate from the face. And they, in turn, supported by the indigo shadow. The woman leans on one full arm; the other curves up and around her – in the same gesture, Estella thinks, as the curving gesture Mercy makes, looking up and out of the basement window. The hand of the curving arm rests on the opposite shoulder. Auburn and black bracelets encircle the arm, at the level of the painted woman's mouth. Estella's painted one of her painted women again, even in her time out. She can still do it: it's vivid; it's good; she's pleased. There is some derivative feel about it. But still it's a good painting of Mercy. Estella looks at it: the painted woman on the piece of book jacket card. Estella wishes she could write a book for her jacket – a book about images of women. It would need to be written, somehow, from the wings – the image of the actress, the model, the prostitute, the dancer; seen from the wings, only half-glimpsed. Someone brightly coloured and barely known or knowable, a woman of secrets like Mercy, or the dancer. But how to prevent a gallery of Andy's Princess Michaels. This, Estella knows, would be the basic problem. You couldn't get between them, in writing: the women and the paint. You would have to use a lot of windows or mirrors, and put other, older images in–ones created by other people. And then, thinks Estella, what about the story? If there was no story, no-one would know what you meant. And then all the work would be wasted. All the same, Estella thinks she could probably do it, one day.

Estella looks across at Mercy. She wears a thin dress of fine silks: a handkerchief dress: a lot of fragments sewn together so that it drapes her like a lot of gypsy's kerchiefs. It's a gypsy woman's dress. Her hair is henna-auburn, her mouth is soft, her eyes are reflective, with waiting – sad, a little. A little misty. Perhaps with the Moet et Chandon. In the late afternoon, the light and the champagne softening and fading, Mercy is pale and soft in the bright room, its colours true to the daylight, filtered by the grey of the city roofs and the city rooms.

Estella looks at her picture. It is darkly vivid and its colours are stark: the daylight filters through in streaks, and the streaks are opaque. The picture has nothing of the day's translucence, nor of Mercy's late afternoon softness. But, thinks Estella in a puzzled way, Mercy has been somehow changed by the picture, into the very antithesis of itself. She looks again at Mercy, leaning, waiting, patiently, on Clive's table: all softly and quietly, in a still, small space among the art work. In the painting, the decadent, the lurid painted woman. At the table, a still woman: a woman of grace and thoughts. The colours of the painting are strong; the colours of Mercy are soft. There is something between them: an edge is set up. What is between, is the change in Mercy. Was it the afternoon that effected it, or was it the painting.

Part Three

Estella arrives back at the dancer's house. She pushes open the old, iron gate, she trails her hand along the black, iron railings. She feels again the dust, all ingrained in the black, sees again the peeling paint, and tries hard to find the decadence it had all promised, there in the decay of it. Tries hard to find the painted underworld she seeks, and pushes to the back of her mind the suspicion that Clive's magenta flock, and the model Mercy actually people that world, not the Mercy of the basement, and the dancer. But the gypsy could come here. He could not go to Clive's apartment. This is a place for the gypsy. There's a smell to the front door. It smells of the great expectations of Estella's first day at the dancer's house, and the damsons. It mocks Estella, and makes her breathe too fast. She takes the huge key, and opens the door.

All the lights are on. The dancer is in her room downstairs, in her chair at the side of the piano, sewing. Estella looks in, and the dancer beckons her in, to sit down. You look a bit weary, she says. All this coming and going, and filthy trains. She says. There's a gin and tonic on the piano and bits of old lace trail the floor. The more Estella looks, the more there is of this lace. It's all tucked under the dancer's chair, as though it shouldn't be exposed to the light. Estella fingers a piece of it: it's all joined together. It's an old, a very old lace dress, in advanced stages of decay. The piece Estella is holding disintegrates. The dancer is sewing it with pieces of thin, black thread. My eyes are too old to see white, she says. And so, the yellowing lace has small spiders sewn into it. This was my wedding dress, says the dancer. It's very derelict now, though. I get it out from time to time, and try to put the bits back together, to stop it falling to pieces completely. I think if I preserve it, someone might like to put it in a museum, one day. I dare say it will be very valuable. It was a very good one, in its day. Very expensive. Very the thing. Estella watches the spiders crawl gradually, gradually over it. Perhaps she should offer to do some of the sewing, in white thread. She fingers another yellowing piece of it. The piece suspended drops into nowhere. Estella decides against offering to help. The dancer seems to know, somehow, how to control it, to keep it together. Of course, says the dancer, I was never married. She gets enormous pleasure from this revelation, Estella can see. She smiles a wide, wrinkly and twinkly smile. Oh no, she says, I was never married. I only wore it for the fittings. Estella leans forward, gently, to ask a silent question. Oh, I changed my mind, says the dancer. Changed my mind the day before. My mother was furious. The local poor children had a feast that day. We had to call it all off, and someone had to eat the food. We couldn't just leave it to rot, could we. Estella thinks they could have. It would have made the right setting – in an old, dark and sombre room. Spread out on the table. And the dancer could have presided, in that dress. Then they could have put the entire scene in the museum.

What happened, asks Estella. Why did you change your mind? I just lost my nerve, I suppose, says the dancer. I just couldn't face it. It was another era, then, you know. Not like these days, at all. It was a ridiculous time for women. We all came out. You never saw such fancy dress in all your life. She has a big swig of the gin and tonic, or perhaps it's just gin, it occurs to Estella, watching the spiders, their legs all awry, finger and crawl over the lace. We had to be all rigged up, laughs the dancer, in tight white dresses pulled in at the waist with strings, and enormous white feathers bowing and toppling from our head-dresses. And then we had to walk into a ballroom balancing all this, and leaning around all haughtily at the other end of it there would be the men, dressed in black, for all the world as if they'd come to a funeral, with white gloves so that if they took our hands we wouldn't get contaminated. The strange thing was, she says, moving in closer to the recollection, that we quite enjoyed getting ready for it; getting all dressed up together in a huge room full of mirrors. We all admired each other and tried on each other's clothes, and then when we were ready we looked at ourselves in the mirror and we really were the bees' knees. But it was when you got there that you felt ridiculous. All these funeral usher individuals used to lean against the walls for all the world as if they were bored to the roots, and give us the once over. You felt as though whatever you looked like they'd find fault with it.

Which one were you going to marry, asks Estella. Oh, good god, says the dancer. I wouldn't have married one of those ninnies. No no, my father was an artist and he had a young apprentice, a sculptor – he did the three women sculpture you can see from your window. And I was going to marry him. But, says Estella who feels as if she is stranded between two unrelated fairy tales – It was the same thing. Says the dancer, as though this explained it. I just knew it would be just the same thing. It was all going to be dreadfully romantic: he would be in his studio, making wonderful sculptures, and I would linger in there wearing something long and romantic, or entertain painters and poets at enormous dinner parties where I served something delicious and talked to them sympathetically about their art. I could just see myself doing it, she says, and Estella leans forward to ask, again, Why . . . Because I couldn't *feel* all that in me, says the dancer. Do you know what I mean? I could imagine exactly the woman I thought I would look like, doing all that, but I couldn't imagine what would happen if I got there and found it was just me, and she'd disappeared. Estella understands this perfectly; and marvels, that someone as old as the dancer discovered it, all those years ago. It would be quite unlike being taught to dance, when the teacher at the front of the class says, Watch me. But don't try to do what I do, because you're facing the other way round. It's like a mirror image. Just watch me, and you'll feel it in the blood. You become the dancer, watching her, Estella knows, in a way that you can't ever become the yourself you imagine for yourself. The dancer, being a dancer, must be particularly aware of the difference.

And so?, asks Estella. And so I got out of it, says the dancer. I called it all off, and while everybody was still in a fluster over it, I ran away. I ran away and caught the boat to France, and lived in a room in Paris. I got a job with a dancing troupe, which was all right. They paid you peanuts but at least it was independence. This is the way the dancer talks. She sums it all up, a whole life-story, in a cliché. But such a cliché, that the magic of it is that it actually happened, to the dancer. Estella might have known. Those feet tell a story. And so, they sit in the twilight together, Estella, and the dancer, musing upon the story so glibly told, now shared. The dancer sews her thin, black thread and Estella looks on, and stores the image of that dress in her mind, the dress that belongs, weirdly Estella feels, to another story, one that would give it more prominence. And yet, whatever the story you invented for that dress, it would still have a strange and mysterious meaning of its own, a meaning in the yellowing lace and the thin, black threads, a meaning that could only be contained in the dress, not in any story.

Estella's room is eerie, that night. The door of her cupboard seems fraught with a secret, as though it might at any moment burst open on the dress. Though Estella knows, because the dancer's music has gone on downstairs, that it's still draped and swathed over the dancer's lap, having its threads put in.

* * *

It's Monday, and Estella gets up to the stillness of a bright sun. There's a brightness in the room; an excitement about being alone, reflected in its textures. It's all all right, somehow, today. Estella wears her blue kimono to go down the stairs, and to open the door onto everyone who's already awake and walking in the early sun. Estella opens the door to get the milk bottles in and she sees the baby's pram outside sunning the baby, and she looks down the steps for Mercy and Mercy waves up, out of the window and Estella feels today has promise. It's one of those days. The Dancer's still asleep. And if the Dancer sleeps late she sleeps very late. The companionship for which Estella earns her living, those magical days out of time, occur at brief and irregular intervals.

So Estella runs upstairs today and washes her face and quickly puts on her thin cotton baggy trousers and a loose shirt, and goes outside and runs. She runs on her flat black shoes like ballet shoes with little low heels. And she feels light as a dancer who's practised for hours and got over the pain and really feels her limbs lift in new and particular ways. She's lighter and lighter as she runs. She runs into the breeze of the dusty pavements where people walk, every day, around and about their lives. She runs over the very pavements people walk over to get their shopping; to fetch their children from school; to catch their trains.

Estella loves the city. She loves the left-over dust of it. She runs on the city pavements light as dust itself, light as little grey threads-of-silk city spiders. And she feels the pavement that shares so many lives. Estella loves the city, because it sees clothes, cast aside. It sees hats and black stockings and silk scarves and suede shoes. It sees people rushing and clashing and making deals, and it also sees the mystery of the dark night over the city lights sparkling on the pavements. Estella likes mystery. She likes the mystery, and the mystique, of other people's lives, because you design your own solutions. You put all the wrong things together. You make a picture out of one person, and another, and you illustrate it with particular clothes, particular fabrics, and particular times of day. In the city, a whole kaleidoscope of textures is thrown together, because there's no space to keep them separate. In the city you make pictures out of glimpses. And you make stories. And you get it wrong. And that's a kind of art.

Estella runs the whole way round the dusty block, and as she runs she gets lighter and her body gets out of breath. But Estella's exhilarated. She runs into the sun and back along the pavement to the mysterious, blue-grey powdery house. And it's still the early morning. When she gets back she bathes and she puts on her perfume and her silver bracelets and she paints her eyelids navy blue and the doorbell is ringing so she drapes the navy blue kimono and in a new world she goes downstairs (the dancer is still sleeping) and opens the door. It's Pip, who's learning to dance. He's little and fair and serious, and he comes to see the dancer from time to time even when he doesn't have a dancing lesson because he likes her. And she lets him watch the television. He's there in the early morning looking up at Estella as though he's got a deal to discuss or a business problem on his hands, and Estella looks right down and tries to treat him as though she's convinced. He's got a holiday from school because it's half term, he says, when she asks. The dancer's getting up, like a mother who hears her baby cry in her half sleep. And it's Pip's birthday. Happy Birthday! says Estella, and she brings him inside and she tells him the Dancer's been asleep but she's getting up now. Pip's going upstairs to see the Dancer, so Estella takes him into the kitchen, instead. And they look out together at the sun. It *is* going to be fine, says Estella. All day, for your birthday. Pip's not sure. There was rain on the weather forecast and so they both look out again. Pip's back in the hall and so Estella opens the front door again, just to make sure it's still sunny, while she asks what he's going to do, on his birthday. The dancer's going to take him out to a restaurant, and he'll have ice-cream, he hopes. He usually can. She took him to a restaurant twice before. Once for Christmas and once for his birthday. Estella's sure it won't rain. But if it did, she's not sure if they'd know by looking out of the back or the front door. She doesn't know, she says, which side the rain comes from. Pip looks into Estella's face. And he says, I think it comes from above. The Dancer's ready. She's coming downstairs, and in her hand there's a little parcel. For Pip. Pip gets a proper watch. With a second hand. And so it's time to go out for ice-cream, and Pip and the dancer go trotting and striding together, and it's a birthday out there in the city, on the pavements, kicking the leaves, scuffling in the dust, the tall, straight figure, and the little happy one.

Estella dresses in bright blues, today. Blue's for risk. Cobalt blue and aquamarine, she wears. A silk shirt that's matt and unyielding to the touch; but so light. Soft and hard, together, as a spider's web. And down she goes. Cobalt blue, to Mercy, who's contrasting magenta in a thin, wrap-over dress the colour of her henna-red hair. Estella is bright with mystery; an off-beat brightness, says Mercy. Where have you been, Estella, asks Mercy. Where are you going, mysterious one. But Estella's just come to see Mercy, and to ask if she found any faces, at Clive's in the white-walled room with the steps, Mercy and Andy. We found bodies. Says Mercy. First I was Colette, draped on the back of a lion. I only had a big rug, so we put small cushions for the ears. Then I had bright pink vinyl limbs and bright green satin limbs and bright yellow sun-beam limbs, and I was a glamorous punk in the jungle. Mercy's not impressed, so they laugh about it. That unimpressed sort of laughing that can be done. Mercy's unhappy. Because she's a fur and darkness and a streak of rather old coloured paint kind of model. In the Sixties she was a bright colours on white. But you can't mix any of those things up, any more. Mercy thinks. You have to do something so new and something people are so ready for that when they see it they think they've seen it before. Like the old furs of the '70s that Sarah Bernhardt had worn. People were so excited by all the furs and feathers and dust and black eyelids that they uncovered all the old sepia photos of Sarah Bernhardt and reproduced them. Because they thought they complemented all the new discoveries. You make art out of its own accessories. That's what Mercy thinks. And she drinks weak coffee out of a big mug which she holds like a beer mug. And doesn't smoke. And Estella and Mercy sit in the window of the basement and look in an out-and-up angle at the sun, and wait for the neighbour who will wheel the sleeping baby away for the day, and care for little Mercy by sitting in the sun feeling happy, and by still feeling happy when the baby wakes up, so that she smiles down at her. Because Mercy's going to her dancing class. Mercy dances without being a dancer, because she's a model. She dances for self discipline and beauty. In a class, just once a week. She dances to feel pain and a burning, a stretching sensation in the backs of her knees. She dances to feel her spine extend, and to feel it breathe and stretch; she doesn't dance for Degas and Picasso and Diaghilev as Estella does. She dances for strength. There's a kind of calm repose about Mercy, with strength behind it. A grace.

Come! says Mercy. Come to the dancing class. Estella is out of practice. And her feet are no longer strong enough. Estella finds beauty in yoga. A static dance, a kind of sculpture which you can grow out of your own limbs and your own breathing. Building a new shape. You sit in a right angle, thighs and knees and calves and ankles on a straight line flat against the floor. You lift your arms in a swoop and a surge upwards; you lift your spine and your shoulder blades in one gesture. And you unfurl down and down, the backs of your knees stretching and stretching until suddenly they're not going to snap any more because they're soft, and you unfurl and uncurl until your head is, softly, softly, touching your knees in a little touching, stroking gesture. In so unfurling you make a new shape for your body, you make a beautiful curve. And if you were made of smooth white stone, which you feel you are, that would be art. No. Says Mercy. That's not good enough on a bright, a bright *blue* day. Go and get your shoes. Says Mercy. And so Estella goes up the stairs past the sleeping baby and out of the brightness into the cool dust of the house and gets her dancing shoes and her leotard and her powder blue tights for dancing. She sings "Happy feet, I got those happy feet" and she's a little black Sambo, dancing upstairs to the sun outside.

Outside in the sun the baby Mercy is awake and clinging to Mercy, and being passed to the neighbour. And she'll sit on the grass in the neighbour's garden and play with little objects and make new shapes with them. And she'll be balanced on the rough stone wall by the neighbour and passers-by will take her soft hands in theirs because it's something special to touch a small baby's hands, which cling to things and hide things and pick things up and put them in new secret places, but which don't know, yet, what it's like just to touch, and linger. So people like to touch the little Mercy's hands and just to linger, there, and so to find a new thing to show the baby. Come on, little one, says Mercy to her baby, and she gives her to the neighbour and she waves a small wave, scaled down for the baby. And down they go, Mercy and Estella, down the road to the bus through the streets past the people past the shops, past the floral gardens past the sea past the banks and the town hall, past everyone going somewhere and some who are just there to be out in the sun, and into the musty hall of mirrors and floorboards.

Everybody practises at the bar and Estella's legs swing with the other legs but not so high. She wants to swing backwards and forwards so that each way all the legs in front of and behind her slither to the floor like falling, pastel coloured dominoes. And with the swing of her thighs she feels the strain in her knee joints and when they swing upwards and down to the ground from the pelvis, like a child's spinning top, then Estella feels the strain and a vague shadow of sickness in the pit of her stomach. Shadows and pressures from another world hover in Estella's body, as the teacher, who's called Ann, stands poised, projecting an actress's voice, her back view reflected behind her in the huge mirror, which shows the pastel line of girls at the bar, a pale blur of pinks and blues, a streak of the Sixties in the painting by Degas from which someone's removed the little fluffy white ballerinas. Now there's a tinny piano playing church hall dance music, and there's all the intoxicating dust and bare-board feeling of an empty stage, with no set, at rehearsal time. And they jump and they swing and they balance on an invisible platform right inside the body, and they make huge movements with all the strength of the back muscles, and they manoeuvre and manipulate little dancing footsteps in complicated and uniform patterns on the floorboards. Like making little miniature paintings out of raindrops. All the time to the clinky music and the clear voice of the darling Ann, there are little intricate, Oriental patterns growing on the dusty floorboards, and big, splashy streaks of movement and colour billowing in the air, and Estella, here in this world, is a tiny drop; a pinpoint; a tear; a little speck of dust, and the shadows of nausea and of a dim strain are growing in her body. Until it's time, briskly, to stop dancing and Ann does a tiny little dance of her own, to stretch, and unwraps the top of her chocolate bar for a nibble at a time, and balances her orange juice on the piano.

Mercy ties her magenta wrap-over dress round her leotard and tights and she's vigorous and refreshed, and Estella's tired. Estella peels off her dancing things and puts on the cobalt and the ultramarine, and she's hot in the hot electric of the blue, and out they go into the steely sun. And the minute Estella gets outside with Mercy on to the street and sees their own radiance against the backdrop of a toytown of stumbling, fading people, Estella's radiant and bright and she's STELLA again, out there in the sun, with magic powers of poise and lights which other women who do not dance will never know. They're two bright streaks on a buff coloured canvas, Mercy and Estella, and Mercy tells her how she *told* her and how Estella is razzle dazzling in the sun and look at the new, bright feelings the dancing has given her. Dancing's like drinking, says Mercy. It depends on how you feel already. If you feel bright, you get very very bright, and if you feel low, you get lower. Estella and Mercy are high, and they go into a wine bar in the bright 5.30 of the afternoon, and drink cold white wine and Estella has a Bucks Fizz because she says she feels like the name of it, with all this sun and this music and this bright, bright lightness.

Dusk. In the dusk Estella leaves Mercy at the basement steps and she climbs the crumbly steps. The house is in darkness and there's the strange, threadbare feel about it that you feel in it when it's empty. Estella goes in and it's dark in the hallway. The dancer's been making ratatouille and the sounds of Stravinsky seep downstairs to the waning smell of French restaurants. The Dancer makes good ratatouille, when she's happy. Or when she's been alone all a long day and she wants to be. Happy, and alone. In through the dancer's kitchen, Estella walks, past the rows of mouldering damson jam nobody eats, there for the dancer to have been able to be stirring jam at midnight, when other landladies, and even other dancers, are asleep in bed for the night. Through the kitchen, Estella walks, out towards the tall glass door at the end, where she looked for the sun, with the little birthday boy. There's a mirror propped bizarrely behind the kitchen door. For images of damson jam and aubergines, bubbling and sizzling in the background when the dancer's hair is down her back, in the evenings. Now there's a tarnished image of Estella, blue and blonde, in the dim room at dusk, just out of the sunlight.

In the dusk in the kitchen, just discernible in the speckly mirror, Estella says, pink martini, or red martini. Softly, to herself. She cracks the dancer's ice, chink into a tall thin glass. There's a whole bottle of red. There's a slosh in the bottom of pink. She has a martini split. She sings, Try a taste of martini, the most beautiful drink in the world, it's the bright one, it's the right one, it's martini. Softly, to herself. It's martini, sings Estella. And there in the dusk the world dazzles again, and Estella's body sparkles cobalt blue, and she's the bright one, she's the right one, it's the dancing, that's made her feel this way. And there's a mood, back again in the sparkly evening. After the hot, bright day. And Estella thinks of the baby Mercy, soothed to sleep beneath her in the basement, and of Pip, snug in a bed somewhere, perhaps, or, (it feels later than it is) glowing happy in a big chair, relating the story of the pink ice-cream he had in a restaurant, with the dancer. And she thinks of the dancer, upstairs, languid in a chaise longue, her ringed hand on the arm, listening to Stravinsky, dreaming of Diaghilev's new dances, and new colours, when all the world of his dancing was new. And she listens to the music, and she discovers, chinking pink ice in the sparkly glass, that the music has changed and it's thinner, and simpler, and it's become the naïve music of a child's playing. Someone is playing the dancer's piano. And Estella chinks the ice and drinks, and hears a Bach prelude, and listens to the purity of the form, and thinks how resonant and pure in its clear simplicity, is such music, in the dusk. And Estella goes up the stairs and there's a new note. It sounds clearly in the still house, and it says "Play". Estella listens again, and it's like the single note of a voice singing. The music slows up and it falters, and the note that sings "Play!" is more strident. Estella stands still quietly and stops her sipping. Notes do not intone their own names, so it cannot, as Estella first thinks it might, be singing the note, "A". It sings it again, and this time it urges, "Play, boy!" (Playboy? thinks Estella) And the notes of the tune are faltering until they cease altogether and the dancer's voice says something Estella can't hear, and Estella hears the dancer move across the room. The Stravinsky on the record starts to play again and the little thin reedy tune has stopped. Estella hears the steps, now, of dancing on the floorboards, thinly muted with old Oriental rugs and mats, and Estella puts her martini down on the ground. For the dancer is dancing. The dancer is dancing and Estella must see the dancing of so many years, enacted in one body. Estella has to see the dancer dance. Is her hair down her back? The dancer, Estella can see it in her mind, will be dressed in the costume of an old dance. She will wear peacock blue for the twenties. She will wear bright blue feathers and ultramarine scarves. She will unfurl and uncurl to the music, remembering how Isadora Duncan danced. Estella sees, before she looks, the dancer dancing towards the death wheels of some strain; some painful memory. Had she, perhaps seen Estella and Mercy dancing on the pavements, radiant and colourful from the dance? The dancer will wear nothing on her feet, Estella imagines, and she softly, softly pushes the door, and it silently opens a little crack.

Pip is seated with his back to Estella, at the piano. The gramophone plays strident Stravinsky. And the naked woman dances Diaghilev. Her body makes the lines, the twists, the erotic and majestic flourishes of Diaghilev's art. The dancer creates invisible silks of flourishing and dazzled air. She flings and meanders and unfurls the shapes of her own body and she is a living sculpture; a moving painting. Estella is still. She stands at the door and she watches the dancer and there's nothing on Estella's face. The pure lines of no expression. The dancer is not seducing a child. The dancer is an artist, with a child as her model, her material, and the impulse of her design. The dancer had not known the pain and the death throes of birth. She had chosen, instead, to control her creation. To take its lines and its textures and direct them into life. She had the dance; in the days when Picasso fathomed and doodled multi-coloured harlequins and clowns. When Isadora Duncan strangled herself in her own dazzling materials, and when everything exploded. Era of kaleidoscope images. And since those days, the colours had faded. No more grease paint, even the parrot watching from its cage is faded. Only the dancer's dancing feet were visible, scarlet tipped, the last traces of her colour, to be seen at the window of the dusty blue-grey house, out there alone, beckoning the sun, on bright, dazzly days. Only the scarlet tipped feet revealed the possibility of a bright-painted interior. Only the very tips of the dancer's body, exposed, told the world there had been scarlet tap shoes and bright cerise satin ballet shoes, with red ribbons; the grease paint; the bare bulbs, the taffeta and net, the heavy red curtains of the stage. Only the feet exposed the last traces of the dancer, painted in glorious, heavy and grease-painted colours, for the stage. Only the feet. Exposed to occasional, observant people, riding by on the tops of buses. And now the feet dance for the small child, seated in silence, watching the show. And Estella, looking on, her eyes following the lines of the woman's limbs, dancing for the child, Estella's gaze is carved for the dance. And Estella is part of the dance and inseparable from it.

Part Four

Estella has a Victorian doll. She lives in Estella's room in the dancer's house: the dead, faded lady with the black pencilled eyebrows. Her dress is of soft, crimson silk and her hair is real. She's a model for a dated femininity, preserved, in wax and china. Her hair is as real and as old as the dancer's; and as unbelievable. Estella calls her Fleur because she's like a pressed flower: preserved, as something precious, though her season is past.

Estella draws Fleur to her on her chair in the dim corner of the room. The angle-poise lamp is green-shaded and rusty as a bench that has been left out in the rain. As rusty as that, and as unhelpful. It doesn't work, because Estella and Fleur have knocked it, one or other or both of them, off the table in the night. In a dream, perhaps. Or more likely, just leaning out an arm to switch off the radio. So that bit of the room is dim. Estella is thick with railway carriage chocolate. Sweet and old. These days when she has been very alone for a whole, hot day, Estella takes the train and she goes one stop to the station. Everyone is waiting for someone. Except the grimy old men, whose coats are torn and whose hair and shoes are dirty. The whole railway station is covered in dirt. Not just the dust of the city, but dirt that smells. So that if you eat chocolate out of one of the dispensing machines on the station, you take dirt inside you. On the magazine stall, there is a belligerent woman, who watches for filthy fingers pawing her magazines. And in her eyes everyone who wants to catch a train is dirty. This is how she makes Estella feel, when Estella strolls up, her chocolate half-opened, to pick a magazine to justify her train ride. And, on these days, Estella watches the people come and go, and notes that people are still there, on the outside of the world, coming and going. And then she takes the next train home again, to see Fleur.

This day it is Sunday evening, and Estella has come all the way back on the train. But it is only a pretend journey, for Estella. She has just been to have been there, so that she could come back. Now Estella is thick with sweet chocolate. Sweet and old. Fleur is soothing in her dryness. Estella closes her eyes, and wonders if there is anything else to reach for, beyond Fleur. Whether there is anything more true and more appropriate as a reward for the achievement of sticking it out, than the little dry puppet-doll. Perfectly autonomous. And therefore, capable of showing where Estella ends. Tears are soothing. Estella licks her tears and they taste of nothing. Even her tears have stopped working. There is no salt in her tears, no blood in her baby doll Fleur, and no light in her lamp. After the night when Estella and Fleur knocked the lamp off the little table, ever after that the corner of the room has been dim. The thickness inside Estella is chocolate stuffing. And so she lies, frail in those days of early morning, growing chocolate silently inside her. Soon she will be fat and swollen, soon people will begin to notice. Estella feels sickly and very heavy. In the dim room, Estella lies, arms around the raggy doll. Estella lies alone, and she doesn't get up and do anything. She lies with her eyes open.

*   *   *

Estella is crying, and when she's started to cry she gets up. She stretches her legs out very straight, first one and then the other, in a dancer's stretch, to the floor. Getting up Estella goes to the wardrobe and she gets out a pair of new, black suede shoes with high heels. Each heel is a tapering cylinder. A slim furl of paper. And the black shoes make Estella walk tall and straight. They are sleek suede to tiptoe and totter on hotel carpets in. Shoes for elegant ankles. Estella brushes her hair. She puts silver pear drop earrings from Paris in her ears. She stands. She paces the room. She lights a small, slim cigar with a small, slim, black lighter – a tapered tube to match her heels. Estella walks, testing her thighs and her ankles. Testing the lines her legs make. She puts on a record. When Estella stoops to solitude, and paces her room again, and again, and so often it feels like forever, she smooths her hair with a practised gesture, and tries to dry away the tears. And poses, anyhow, to mask the pain. Estella, breathing slowly, Fleur clinging raggily, moves to the window, her cigar posed, her stilettos poised, and Estella looks out and waits. The gypsy might come today. She sent him a card, from the railway station. So he knows where to come, if he should want to, after all this time.

Outside the Dancer wears a matted wool sweater, and torn trousers. Her hips are too wide, in the trousers, for her tapered, Dancer's ankles. Her feet are too long. Through broken sandals cracked toenails are crimson. Her hair is somehow stuck about the matted sweater. The sleeves have lost their cling. The clothes distort the lines of the dancer's body. Make a parody, a masque of it. And dipping, dipping a matted brush into tacky paint, she streaks the fence scarlet on dirt, and Estella, looking out, splinters, somewhere in her face, the faint traces and beginnings of a painted scream. You see the lines begin to form. Estella clutches and clings Fleur tighter, but she is dry and cold. Estella feels a splintering, low in her stomach. Fleur is silent against Estella's body, and she has no heart to beat against Estella's breast, no little movement to soothe or still the splintering. Estella brushes the china forehead with the flutter of a kiss. She caresses the doll. The tears are splintering, spilling, pulsating, and outside the window the Dancer streaks smears of scarlet on grime, streaks colour lurid over the splinters. Estella's still watching, and she sees a child and its mother pass by in the early morning, quickly, to get to school. The child says, Why is that lady so *dirty*? And the mother says, sshh, the lady is painting so she has her old clothes on because she doesn't want to spoil her nice new ones. What *dirty* clothes, says the child, what a *horrid* lady, and they pass by on the other side of the street. The Dancer smiles secretly, and goes on smearing the fence scarlet. Estella and Fleur lean, tearful and papery, against the dusty window, closing their eyes, silently. Clenching their tears.

* * *

Through the city night Estella walks. Swiftly past the cinema, past the gaudy Bingo Hall. Veering round the old couple, briskly past the local lads. One grimy yellow waste bin leers a huge slot for your dirt. Estella passes close by it. The city is flashing its Saturday night lights and makes faces look sickly. Headlights veer in the dark cold. Estella bites into the cold with her steps. The cold is so crisp you could bite into it. It could bite you. Past Marks and Spencers, bleak in the darkness, Estella clips in high shoes. Shoes high, slim and prim beneath a black shiny coat, belted tight. Estella's face is round with cold. It loses any expression, braced against the dark. Walking and walking, thrusting through the slicing cold, pushing out into the dark the constricting memories of the film she has just seen hoping to discover a new-coloured world to want to be in. And instead, finding the darkness and fear of others before her in glorious technicolour, reminding her: it is all real. And it is not only real, it is art. You could make art out of fear, and that alone makes Estella more fearful. Stevie Smith, was the film. Estella is frightened of such stoicism, sustained until death. Stoicism frightens Estella, more than all the guns and fires and air crashes in the world. Not waving, but drowning Estella might almost be herself, as she waves obligingly to a passing car honking and leering and beside itself with fun, drunken men falling all over and all out of it, to see a solitary woman in a real night on a real pavement, out of the movies. What larks. Drowning, she briskly strides. Her hands are in her pockets and the cold makes her eyes water. Baffled, he swung backwards. Recited Estella from her favourite novel, to soothe, and to arouse in her mind pictures of golden yellow grapes of Greece, and a golden glow of loving, out of a novel. Novels have colours, and Estella remembered a yellow novel, to sun her and to soothe. She strides and strides. Past the gangs on their motorbikes, past the *King and Queen*, with its plaster king and queen. Cast in a plaster heart, Estella walks bravely and the streets become more solitary, leaving the rocking and flashing of the city behind. And walking becomes more strenuous but dizzying, rushing as Estella now is on a false energy. Cars pass.

Suddenly there is a wrench. Estella is still walking and the wrench puts the climbing, clamouring plants and the cultivated beds and the tennis courts, puts this all in dreamland, and all that is real is a white car on the road beside her. It's as if it has struck her: so sure is Estella of her place, as its victim. The car is white and it flashes silver metal. Titillated, the body work gleams. There is a wrench. A grey knot. The road is black, and everything is pitch. Cars are speeding, certainly with no-one inside them, and Estella is lurched out of the world of darkness into a new, an artificial black. Everything shimmers. Estella listens for the night owl and there is no sound. On the road, cars hoot, gangs hang out of speeding windows. To the left of Estella, bordering the pavement, big chasms of gateways with their rusty metal numbers and dusty leaves, make a shading as a backdrop to the bright, dark road. The houses are empty, some derelict, Estella is alone. Not drowning but dry inside. Primly she minces, hoping to ward off danger by emanating the cold empty space of spinsterhood. To show: there is nothing there. She is empty spaces. A face looms and leers beside Estella. The voice says, Why don't you come with me, lady. It speaks. Estella listens to the sound of the voice. Pitched quite high, and Spanish. Estella says, No. She just says no and she keeps walking. The car pulls away. The voice spat, the car sped, into the night. Why didn't the night owl cry, Well done? Why did not the night owl croon, It's O.K?

It's O.K., says Estella, to herself. It's all right, darling, says the striding Estella, to the little curling, crying Estella she feels inside. And they walk together, the two lonely ones, soothing each other with empty soothings, false promises. Two Estellas. On the dusty road, there in the bright, dark city. In the night owl's night; skirting the heart of darkness which is that wrench; that grasping tightness, that desperate constric tion of not being able to make changes, where all is not right. All. Estella smooths her nerves with automatic hand and there is the white car in the gutter again.

There is the white car in the gutter again – Estella looks away – still there, – Estella looks back. Estella walks on and on in the darkness and each step is a heart beat, as automatic and as inevitable. Estella will stop walking when the heart-beat stops. She's walking to keep living. The car is in the gutter. The park is to the right. And it goes on in a space to the right for miles and for no-one to hear. On the left, the comfort of rooms, where garments brushed walls and people talked and babies were born and life went on, and went on changing. The comfort of style, in clearly delineated and partitioned spaces. So you knew where you were. Estella kept close to the edge of the houses. Suddenly there was a face. Close by her side. When she looked again it was still there. The smile on the face was proud and malicious. It gleamed all the spite and the ease of something to kill her. A superhuman irritation. A self-righteousness in that face, at Estella's expense, to violate her whole body, just with its conceit alone. Why at her expense? And, where was the face diverted? What was the face doing? What was the automatic hand, . . . Estella did not register the view exposed by the unzipped trousers. The houses all had their lights off. The houses were in darkness. Estella was alone, exposed to the darkness, and the smile of the man. Estella saw malice, triumph, vulgar cruelty, Estella saw all the spite she would ever see, there in that face. Ha ha ha said the hand of the flasher. Ha ha ha said the surreal grin, somehow lit up, in the dark night. Estella turned to the man, turned her whole body towards him. Estella coldly shouted. She said, You bloody . . . She had no noun. There wasn't anything. The man was nothing.

There was no essence of person in this man. The man was the smile. And she couldn't, how could she, have said, You bloody smile.

Estella walks slowly up the steps to the powder blue house. Deferentially. So as not to disturb anyone. Gentle footsteps to make patterns in the sleep of sleeping people. Estella turns on one bright light and sits in the dim room adjacent to this light, in the hallway. There is a cupboard in the kitchen at the end of the hallway. The one with the tarnished mirror propped up behind the door. Estella has her back to the mirror. She creeps to the cupboard and opens it, click, softly. She slides a round lid away from a round tin, and air is expelled. Softly, softly, Estella heavily lifts out the Christmas cake. She balances the whole cake on its edge, and pulls a large, dark, squashy raisin from its base. It's black, and it tastes richly of brandy. Almost, of cigars. The wrench is still grey in a knot inside her. She knows her face, were she to look at it, would be grey. She sucks raisins, to soothe, until her mouth is all brandy and now the cake is pitted. She scratches a piece of icing with her fingernail. A snowflake kisses her and spills a dust of sugar on her tongue. She gets a carving knife and cuts a huge wedge of cake. She pushes as much as she can of the soft, powdery, sticky, heavy brandy cake, with its slice of leering yellow, into her mouth. She pushes so much cake into her mouth that she can't chew. She has to feel the bulk of it and the taste of it. She has to have too much in her mouth. She needs to bite, hard, Estella stuffs cake. She forces it inside her. There's a clock in the kitchen, and Estella watches the hand move, and she pushes and forces and sucks and chews cake for an hour. Swallowing cake her stomach gradually makes clouds which obscure the wrench. It makes clouds of pipe lagging in her stomach and Estella starts to feel a sickly pain clouding over in the place of the wrench. The wrench is now a cold feeling in her neck. Her stomach's swathed in cake, it's a small bullet, secreted in a pudding, like a sixpence. Not real money; not a real bullet. Estella picks up the rest of the cake in both hands. She squeezes it between her fingers. Then she goes out in the dark, down the steps and into the garden. Estella crouches down so that her knees really are on the ground. She feels it, hard and cold, against them. And she digs a hole in the soil with her fingers. And she buries the cake. Then she goes back in the house. She takes a cloth and she cleans the table. She rinses the cloth, and she puts the tin away in the cupboard. She washes the knife, and she puts the knife away. Then she goes up the stairs to bed. In the bed, Estella gathers Fleur to her and her whole body's swollen. Estella reaches for the little, hard body of the doll, and she pulls the china arms around her neck.

But Estella cannot sleep. A curtain in her body pulls itself across, half way, but it is too thin. Her body craves a curtain of crimson velvet. To muffle her screams. And yet, Estella is silent. Her body a whole web of taut strings, a tangle of thin threads. Estella dreams of the man who strides in the sunlight, and kisses the little French girls to sleep in dreams. In the movie of Estella's dreams, Estella sits on a rusty bench in the cold and thinly sunny morning, in her room in the dancer's house.

The gypsy is here. He strides in, up the stairs of the grey blue house and he's Tom Waits on the cover of *Blue Valentine* and he's bronzed and he's strong, and he's unsmiling. Striding mean. Estella's been sitting in the hot sun wearing a navy blue taffeta skirt, gloriously inappropriate for the heat, and her legs are bare. Estella's playing at call girls. Her hair is new-washed blonde for something good to happen. Estella says Do you want a drink. He says, No. I want you. On the floor Estella lies back and loves him, with all her heart. It says in the sub-titles. With all her gypsy romance. Oliver Reed sticks a sword in a dying body. Tom Waits slings a red-shod lady blonde in tatters of taffeta over his shoulder. A cave man drags a woman in a leopard skin by the hair. Dirk Bogarde, as a business man, bangs his fist on an office desk. The door of a Lotus Elan slams. The door clicks, and Estella's lying alone on the bed and she cries as though she will lose her mind. She claws at the bed and she cries all the shock of a gesture; a fling; a thrust; a cruel stroke of paint which defaces a whole canvas. Estella wakes up crying. She lies on the floor, Estella, all through that afternoon, and says, I want you back. . . . Into the air, for the gypsy to hear. She says it over and over and in the end her eyes are too gravelly to show the tears welling, still, in her stomach.

Oh, why don't you come? calls Estella to the gypsy. Oh why don't you come?

* * *

Estella feels elated, this evening. It had seemed to her in a shadow at the back of her mind that the flasher belonged somehow in the scheme of things. This had disturbed her by drawing her back from things – making her feel unduly tired. The flasher belonged, it had seemed to her, somehow in the same space as the miscarriage. In an unruly and potential hell of chaos that would give the lie to the existence of Mercy and the dancer. There was a definite connection between these things: the flasher and the miscarriage was on one side; Mercy and the dancer were on the other. The nature of the thread that held them together, Estella dared not imagine, nor try to envisage. And so, she must re-orientate herself so as to avert herself from the problem. When she felt elated, Estella knew that this reorientation was beginning.

Estella is elated, this evening, early but already dusk, there, in the spice of it: the dusk, drawing in on the late afternoon. And so, she goes to her wardrobe. Opening the door, she smells the faint fragrance, the dull perfume, of Estella. The clothes brush her face and the smell of them is musty, faintly perfumed, and soothing. In the clothes, in the faintly musty perfumed smell, there in the slice of the dark, hung about with cobwebs of clothing, Estella breaths the fragrance of Estella. And is disconcerted by it. In this strange way, Estella stands in the dark and confronts herself.

*   *   *

Estella's still there in the wardrobe, reflecting, and in the wardrobe there's the odour of Estella and of the dust. Estella in the house; the spiders in the wardrobe: all the interiors of Estella's dusty setting, and she, interiorised, trying to get inside them. There in the darkness. There in the darkness Estella runs her hand along her own batwings of clothes. Jutting out, brushing her shoulders, the shoulder blades of wooden and wire hangers. Padded. Estella, in among her own garb. Refusing it light or space by blocking the way out. Sharing its darkness, and its spaces. She caresses the shoulder of each garment, thin slivers and blades of dark cloth. Taffeta, cotton, muslin and silk; velours, and true velvet. And she selects.

Aha, says Estella, I will be a pierrot; a marionette, a puppet, like Fleur. She selects a one piece outfit with harem trousers and tight cuffs with frills, an outfit such as clowns wear. The legs are so circular and so billowy, the ankles so tight, that it makes Estella want to dance. She's light on her feet, dancing tap, but without the sound. The tips of her toes, scarlet-edged, her firm heels, the front edge of her foot, brushing the floor; her feet make sharp little brushing movements, and she's as light as if someone else were pulling her strings. She wears a black and gold bangle, high on her fore-arm, just beneath the elbow. And folds her hair, high at the back of her head, and secures it with a big, red pin. And then she stands still. She walks silently across the room, down the corridor, and takes the left turning into the dancer's room. Moves quickly behind the door; steals a look in the speckled mirror. Too garish, she looks. Altogether too loud. She goes back to her room, pulling out the red pin as she walks. Her hair falls in one heavy movement down her back. So now she's peering in her own small fragment of mirror, the one over the sink, putting on scarlet lipstick. Lipstick for puppets: their grease-paint. Just checking, just proving, it was all too much. She unpeels, unbuttons, lets fall, the marionette suit.

Lifts each foot, one by one, out of the heap of it, on the floor. She tries the taffeta skirt, instead, tests its weight against her naked skin. The taffeta skirt is enough, she thinks. Not too much; just, enough. She finds a tight, black top, like a leotard, for dancing. She stretches it over her. It is enough.

She goes down the stairs into the night dark, she clicks the front door behind her on the house. Her heels are high, and the skirt swings in the night. The heels, thus, are fixed to her – she directs them. The skirt is not. This, she feels, is right. The skirt swings lightly against the curves of her dancer's calves. Hard, with the dancing. She knows this, too, is acceptable. She's in the city, and its lighting flatters her, there, where the world is on stage. Here, there is everything. The lighting, the actors, the audience, and a special, measured time. Here there is movement, and at midnight there will be a curtain. It's all arranged. The show is up. Here is the city. Estella's on. Behind every door you enter, in the shadowy corner of every bar, martini at your elbow, and in your breasts, the promise of a new start. Estella reaches the door. Here she must enter. Here they will all be. The shadowy ones, and the gypsy. Estella's arrived; she's on. But she cannot go in. Her legs will not take her in; her heels are too high. And, after all, her body is attached to them. She cannot enter, there where they will all be waiting in a circle, watching her entrance. The magenta ones and he, and the women. Watching. She can't go in because she's alone. No-one is with her. No-one substantiates her entrance, offers a meaning for it with their presence. No-one's there in the wings, seeing her on. And so they'll all know she's alone, and notice the size and the pure stillness of the space she moves in. And feel the pain of it. People push past her. Estella turns and walks in the other direction. Away from the bar; away from the city; into the darkness; back to her room. Because she can't trust the outside to throw back the same face as the one she saw in her mirror. And is afraid the women will notice: that, there is the night, and now, here is Estella. And: that between Estella and the night, there is nothing but make-believe.

Part Five

In the dancer's bedroom the bed is unmade; the dancer was in a hurry. All the same, the room is practically bare. The dancer does not fling and toss her stuff everywhere. The dancer is sparing with her possessions. It's as though the room's neatly upholstered. No stuffing leaking out. This much, Estella notices, wandering the room listlessly, in her blue kimono. Estella wonders about the dancer's image of the dancer. She wonders how the dancer knows who she is: the mirror is so utterly tarnished. Black spots and streaks, all over it. And a fine glaze over it like dust. Estella looks, and sees a vague shadow of herself, all streaked with black, tarnished marks. Estella, behind and beyond the streaks of black, where the surface of the mirror is peeling. And Estella wanders in the room, and looks around for clues to the real image of the dancer. She opens drawers, and in them she finds tiny paintings. Miniature portraits, in water-colours. And the dancer's passport in which the dancer's photo defines a new dancer. An old dancer, or, rather, in the arrested world of the photo, the young dancer. Bigger and brighter, and more solid. But a distorted image: the mirror is tarnished. All this Estella finds, in the room. A new, a substantial face in a drawer. But a distorted image. Tarnished with time.

Estella lingers and lingers and looks in drawers and touches and feels the fabric of the quilt on the bed, and Estella, there in the dust of the faded room, tries to identify the dancer. Estella, herself, imageless, because of the tarnished mirror, and the dust on its surface. And there is something else missing; some other hollow. A silence, for no-one. People have to have noise. The raw edges of it, and the autonomy of it, cutting the air. This much Estella knows. The dancer could dance to Diaghilev, but only to the Stravinsky of Diaghilev. Not to the silence. Silent images. Swallowed up in the vortex. Sound identifies that process. So Estella's thoughts are running, there in the dust. Trying to sum up. Trying to identify. To find an equation. For the space she finds herself in. Lush in her blue kimono. Making sense of the shadows. Thinner already, from the resolution to be thin. From inventing a new norm for herself of size and shape. A new size; a new shape. As on the canvas. But, the absence of a clear image, in the mirror.

Estella, to clarify things a little, to add a touch of colour, a streak of paint, goes to her own room and brings out her nail varnish. The red. The scarlet. And, puts on some music. The sound will carry through the wall. Loud. To fill the spaces. Her room, and the dancer's. Her own space, and the dancer's. Sitting on the bed, to jazz, Estella paints the tips of each finger and each toe and the hard edges of her are licked with a vivid light. The outer edges of Estella. Daubed ragged red. Jazz borders. To identify the exterior, and show that there's another, a muted secret space. Inside Estella. And, so sitting her legs out straight, her back arched over, applying the scarlet borders to the inside of Estella, Estella, a marionette, the strings slackened, relaxing in the wings, Estella, swathed in a muted blue, applying the red, takes up space in the dancer's private room. And wants to represent this, to better effect.

Estella steps down from the bed, and opens a cupboard, and there it is. Estella pulls out the yellowing lace, cloud by cloud, cobweb by cobweb of it, shred by embroidered shred, the swathes of faded wedding dress. And spreads it out before her on the floor. It's all tarnished, like the mirror. Dappled with faded age and dust. With the shadowed traces of moth and the spiders' black threads: and the little fragments, the little decayed and shadowy spaces in the fabric, these make dapples of fine misted black. Opaque, like the dapples on the mirror. Defying transparency. Not letting you see through. Just, making it visible. The absence of a medium. Unrepresented. Estella smiles, a wrinkled smile all spidery, to herself.

Estella smiling, softly coaxes and gently pushes the blue kimono over her shoulders. The tarnished mirror reflects: smooth shoulders and faded breasts. Faded with the dust of the mirror. Firm and faded. Muted colour, and a stronger, muted colour. But where the colour deepens, you feel the strength, the hardness. And Estella drapes musty lace, soft but stiff with the dust, over her smooth shoulders, her muted breasts. The dress is spread out on the floor, the skirts dragging in the dust, rough on the floorboards, shredded, held together by threads, white confetti, left to wither on the pathway. A dress of dust and confetti. Forever new, and yet so old. Estella spreads the dress so that the stiff bodice stands up by itself, though keeling over somewhat, lacking the stiffness preserved in the skirt, and Estella slides into it, scarlet-tipped toes first. She slides her knees, her thighs, her curving bottom downwards and meanders her way into the cobwebs and as she does so pulls the bodice of the dress up and up, standing, past her waist and up, past her breasts and over her shoulders. Estella pushes her arms gently into the decaying sleeves and she stands, before the tarnished mirror. By leaning and curving round she can do up most of the little pearl buttons; by arching her back and twisting round or by lifting her arms high behind her and pushing the fabric up through her fingers. Only some of the buttons are now left undone.

When Estella walks, she rustles. The music stops at the end of the record, but Estella rustles against the silence. The dancer's room ticks its own rhythm. Tin on tin. Estella slowly moves, and as she walks one little web of decaying fabric falls, disintegrating, flutters away like a feather and the dress falls, slightly, all of it downwards. Estella feels the fabric on her shoulders, pulling all the weight of the dress, just a little, downwards. She goes to another of the dancer's drawers. And she finds two rings. Coral, set in gold. And a big turquoise. Estella fingers the opacity of these. These, thinks Estella, are to jewels as death is to life. Opaque. Like the specks of the mirror. Not reflecting. Not representing. Not able to throw back their piece of the image. Estella slides, over the tips of scarlet, onto slim fingers, the old jewels and she loves them. Estella gets out of her mind in this way. She adorns her body, and takes on the images and textures lent her by the decaying fabrics. Someone else's fabrics and someone else's old jewels. Wearing someone else's faded dress, evoking the faded years of its decay. There, she feels free.

Estella, so freed, rustles and lingers on the stairway. She leans dustily, madly over the edge, and calls to the gypsy. Will you come today, asks Estella, will you come to the door and kiss me on the stairs? Will you caress me, my clothes soothing your fingers with their softness, brushing them softly? Will you come in the sun to the crumbling house? Will you ring the doorbell and then, with no space between the sound and your coming, be kissing me and caressing me on the staircase, where I had been sitting in a navy blue skirt, draping my calves, its colour too dark for the heat of the day? Will you follow me up the stairs, eyes on my gypsy ankles, wanting to gather me up, crumple me to you? A poppy, crumpled and faded scarlet, lies forgotten where someone had picked a radiant and deeply vivid flower of blood, a streak of deep brightness in the canvas of a hillside. Will you pick me today? Asks the scarlet Estella; and the house echoes, ever so slightly, since the floorboards on the staircase are bare, the tilting, leaning, tanned Estella, swathed in the remains of the wedding dress. The stairs themselves, faded, decayed, as the dress itself. Will you? Estella leans over the staircase rail and calls the gypsy. The door does not open. The name drops into the spacious silence; into the spaces between the floorboards.

The front door is shut and no-one is coming, and so Estella tiptoes down the staircase, unevenly, dragging the dress, and at the bottom she goes into the dancer's room. There where are: the piano; the dish of mint-dust chocolates. The faint odour of the must of decay. Estella peeps in, she smiles. She smiles because in the room with the piano, and the faded chocolates, is the parrot in its cage. The opaque turquoise of the jewel, and the coral, these are its colours. Stolen from another era. Another art. O, the erotica, o, the exotica, of decay, sings Estella to herself. She sits among all the vestiges of a life in which fabrics were different, women's faces were different, and different things were usual and familiar. We know these things only by their dust, and believe the past was a shrouded place. A muted space. Such things, Estella ponders on, with the parrot, and the dress, for her accessories. Estella's swathed and at the same time hidden in the lace of another decade; protected from the observers outside the front door. Taking on an image, scarlet bordered, of decay, and so relinquishing her responsibility to an image the world outside will accept. Hidden as if in the very confines, the very interior interiors, of the looking glass. She seeks escape, the eccentricity of the mirror image, wanting to face it: face to face. The lips too red, the eyes too bright, the hair too matted, the fabric of the dress, too decayed. Estella wants to see all this, and to see Estella; and then to seek her reflection in the glass and find it muted, greyed and in shadow. Too much for the world; too much for the mirror.

And Estella, so escaping, so exploring, seats herself at the piano and plays. She plays gently, gently, she runs her fingers over the keys, ever so lightly. She plays one half of a duet: the upper, the clear and reedy half. Le Jardin de Dolly. All clear as a pool it sounds, in the shade. The slim fingers run over the keys all edged scarlet, and muted with coral and turquoise. Over the black on white. The other hand, she rests in the folds of the yellowing dress, in her lap. The dancer's parrot lingers, his head to one side, as though suspended between a choice of worlds, his eye dulled, having ceased for some eras to flutter and fuss. Haunted. His eye dimmed, caged off from the keyboard, not hearing the sound. Estella's faded audience, dull as the wedding dress. Dull as the dust of the room and the chocolates. Dim as the past Estella lingers among, for her titillation. To the strains of Fauré Estella thinks she inhabits a Renoir painting. Or she is Sarah Bernhardt, draped among the furs and hangings of her mysterious room: a touch macabre, and exotic. Estella thinks about the lives that once had colour and movement, and brings them back into the room. Sharing their present by imagining, Estella dresses in the fabric of their time, brings them back a little. Dying a little, embracing decay. Luxuriating in it. Dressing up. And so, Estella undoes something, thought to be resolved. She misses them, Renoir and Sarah Bernhardt, they leave a gap, a silence. Like the gypsy. Estella distorts life, a little, the better to test out her imagination. To create a set for its awakening, to give it presence.

The sharp edged papa whose black patent shoes can be heard crunching on the gravel. Mercy with the scarlet legs, the scarlet backs of knees. The wedding dress. Even the dancer. These, for Estella, represent, signify, decadence. Deviation, she revels in. She swathes herself in the frail threads of lace, made of the webs of spiders, just as the dancer sucks crimson in the night. They luxuriate, Estella and the dancer. They remain in the wings, seeking an underworld. Backstage, they seek old chocolates, red satin and the night. It makes them feel beautiful, it makes them feel daring. For Estella, in seeking the dancer's fabrics, and her old chocolates, and her wedding dress, searches in the dark for a secret. She sees it half lit, and she would paint it scarlet, but keep it hidden. Nurturing a something, half lit and painted scarlet, in the underworld inside her, she would keep it safe in her heart and in her body. Seeing it there, and loving it, and recognising it, in the clothes and the rooms of other people, she knows it's hers and she wants to live it through. To be present in it. But there's another thing Estella wants, and it seems this thing is incompatible with the half light, the scarlet and the damson, the spidery light, of her play. A thing incompatible with the being-in-rooms Estella seeks and finds and plays out, there in the dust, there with the dancer, there with the spiders. She seeks credibility. And for this, she knows, there has to be a renunciation, a denial of the very thing closest to herself, and yet at the same time making the closest thread between her and a world that sparkles with being alive. The thread that she sees the exposed canvas with, the thread that treads thinly between the floorboards and her feet. The thread that connects Estella and the baby, the thread that connects Estella and the dancer. That thread will be broken, by the silent audience, who pass Estella's window every morning, their shoes gleaming, their brief cases slotted into the image of outside, like the black keys among the white. They, all following in slim lines, the path of the sleek, black papa in the Alfa Romeo, do not see Estella. They do not know she is there. She watches them from the window where she is dressed in the wedding dress, or sometimes in tight, taut taffeta, her heels scratch and there are bones in her dress thrusting her body into curves and lines that leer and cut like a knife and her eyes are so heavy with makeup that they are closing with false promises. She dresses to be their toy, they could pull her out of their black brief cases right now and she would perform for them, she would dance in the street. But they do not see her, because now is the time to board the train, and there is no red light at Estella's door. And, anyway, she is on the other side of the window. Just for no reason in the bright morning, there, safe in the dancer's house, with the door closed. Playing in the early light, playing in the shadows. There, in the shade, with the spiders. Estella loves it, is in love with this all. Oh, the femme fatale, Estella. Hidden in the house on the other side of the glass, for no-one to see.

* * *

Through the net curtains, at the basement window, everything is reduced; is shadowed to rectangle and tarnished dapple of hedge leaves, all skirting and tipping pathwards. Shadows of falling confetti. Faded. Through such tarnish, the colours are muted; opaque; a sepia Autumn. Tissue of fog. To the left an apricot rose peeps, to the right garlic whispers: someone is cooking. Mercy is cooking in the basement. There's meat, magenta and livid, in her hands, and salad bowls of oil and crisp leaves. The fingers arrange the colours, they douse more leaves and petals and fragments and shapes of colour, in fresh water. There in the water, the pieces sparkle. A pink rose in a vase on the mantelpiece brushes the dingy wall. On a chair at the window the baby's clothes, crumpled and draped. On the wall above the mantelpiece, a picture of a woman in a garden. On a chair, with a rose coloured cover, a leather purse, with some coins spilling out of it. And a piece of paper. On the table an aubergine and a banana; pencils for the eyes; a bottle of varnish, a bottle of ink. She stands, leaning against a cupboard, an apricot Mercy, pale for thoughts and interiors. Soft as the fruit. She mixes pale yoghurt in a little carton. She cuts up the banana into small pieces. She peels one of the pieces and mixes soft banana into the mixture. She has a small piece of yellow cheese which she cuts into slivers and shavings with the edge of a knife. She eats the shavings herself, sliver by sliver. Then she spoons the yoghurt, spoonful by spoonful, into the baby's mouth. And into her own soft mouth. As she tastes it she reflects: she is an Irish woman, wild with thick, rich chestnut hair in a full, scarlet skirt. Wild on the bare hills in stiletto heels. Running home over the hills in her red skirt and her very high shoes, to write a symphony. She is a dyed-peroxide blonde, all pink fluff and plastic, snatching a quick moment to apply her lipstick in the back of a van: life on the road. She is a woman with straight horizontal lines across her forehead and grey threads in her hair, in a tailored black jacket and good leather boots who rushes, a file under her arm, in the busy grey of eight in the morning, pulling a smartly uniformed but very small child by the hand. She eats some more. She sifts the papers on the table by her and lifts the baby's clothes, garment by garment, looking for something. There are a lot of choices. You can be any number of women. But it's futile to choose. Because once you realise there's a choice, you have to be all of them. Mercy spoons the mixture into the baby's mouth. There is a newspaper on the floor. She picks it up, and reads the article. A woman with children writes about being a woman. Everywhere in print, ponders Mercy, women write about being women. Women with children write about being women and women without children write about being women, while all the time women being women, who neither know nor care about all the print, shop in the supermarket and tip packets of dehydrated dust over pans of water and clear up, and make whole days of all this without apparently feeling the slightest pang, the slightest twinge of guilt, about whether it's allowed: whether it's enough. She moves to a flat chest of drawers and from the top drawer takes out a flat box of chocolates. The baby squeals. She spoons another spoonful. She peels off a silver wrapper.

Estella, languid at the piano in the dancer's room, leans over and stretches her arm, rustling and crackling the dress, to the dish of dusty chocolates. She crunches her teeth on a powder of mint-dust. Mercy, in the basement, tastes a new, soft chocolate of apricot cream. And now the apricot Mercy's remembering, to the taste of the chocolate, how only a short while before, in this very room, she wanted to write poetry, and enter it for a competition, but the gypsy was in the room. Running home, knocking loud and quick on the door at three in the morning to wake her. But she was up, writing her poem. He cutting a line in the room so that the two halves fell to the ground like a garment, pushed from the shoulders, crumpled in a heap either side of her on the floor. She wouldn't have won, anyway. Though she might if the room had been left intact, with the poem on the table, had not been cut in two. And so, at four, or five, his clothes in a heap on the floor and the half light of the early morning trying, weakly, to light up the room as it had been, the poems visible again on the table, but the gypsy in the room and she wanting only and above everything to be alone. But not that alone. Because she loved the gypsy. What she really wanted to do was to be able to distinguish: the gypsy on the one hand; the poems on the other. Until later, the room was bright again with three women, there were voices all through it, and one of the girls looking at her, her mouth, somehow, set, saying, You're not yourself when you're with him. But this time it was the end. He had to belong to her, he had to be real, because of the way he cut the room in half. He was hers the way the room was hers when she saw it spread around her and she seated in it, in her mirror. And then he in the room again in the vivid light of day, knocking the women into the shadows of it as though they were skittles and arguing some point. Saying you know what I mean, don't you. You see what I'm talking about. To her. Wanting an ally but striving, at the same time, to contend. The woman with the set mouth was staring at her and she didn't see why she had to acknowledge a particular choice that seemed to be pushing itself forward, thrusting its way in. The poem or the gypsy – that was right. But she wanted the women, *and* the gypsy. But they were all looking at her and seemed to need to know. She said no. Hoping the girl would, later, tell her why this was the right answer for the room, there, with that particular selection of people in it, and meaning YES. YES. The door slammed. He was gone. And she knew she had transgressed a rule and that he would not come back. And she felt always that that incident had set a precedent, and had identified her with empty space, and doomed her to be alone, because people in real relationships said Yes, Oh, yes; yes, of course. She wanted to have a daughter, just her own, to see their faces. But, it had altered her vision, her perspective, blocked out her old imagination, so much so that even had they made their faces, she wouldn't have been able to make sense of the shapes they made, any more.

*　　*　　*

Estella still lingers, looking out of the window, her elbow rested on the keyboard. Her fingers lingering, the notes small, thinly strident, like jewels in the dust, Estella plays. Looking at her seated there you would see a medieval face. Painted coral or turquoise, reflecting nothing. A flat, an unsparkly face. Pale with a faded pallor – a very old canvas. Only the eyes are pools. Reflecting movement, and Estella's ruminative thinking. The eyes of a mirror. No trace of tarnish. Now, though, as she lingers, making thin tears. Estella's crying softly and wearily. With a calm grace. The tears make a saltiness – it almost seems on the inside, of her pale smooth face, which reminds her body that it is swathed in a dusty lace with the graininess, against her skin, of tears. Moreover, it does not fit. So restricted, Estella cries the frustration of an abstraction she cannot altogether identify. Wanting, above all, to feel connected to something which escapes her. And so, draping textures against her skin, tipping scents from an old bottle, piling colour on colour. Draining yourself (as now, in the wedding dress), of colour. Sitting at the piano, as now, swathed only in folds of lace, her tears and the lace a medium, creating synthesis for an abstraction. Dressing it up. But there's nobody there to read the signs; Estella's all alone and she cries for her solitude. She can't stand the silence so where there isn't a disco, or a main road, Estella talks out loud. Sets words to her music, sets the sign language of her stray notes to literature. She turns the pages of the dancer's library book, which she has left on the piano, and reads a passage. 'Love is blind devotion,' sings Estella, being Miss Havisham, 'unquestioning self-humiliation, utter submission, trust and belief against yourself and against the whole world, giving up your whole heart and soul'. This is what Estella wanted. To feel such things. If only someone had let her; been there to see. And, recognised the signs.

And there in the shadows, Pip, wide-eyed, looks silently on. A real audience, there in the background, a sudden unexpected observer. A child's face can register pure surprise, a hiatus of nothing in his mind, because it makes, just for a second, no associations. There is nothing quite like this, yet, in his memory. And so, on the small face, sheer absence, pure surprise, which sets him apart, signifies his exclusion. The little silent observer sees the wedding dress and notices a tear in it, where Estella's heart is, and gazes on the dust and on the woman, and smells a fustiness, a mustiness given off by the dress, and, turning, trots back away along the corridor, identifying incorrectly the strange figure of a woman he has seen, transfixed for a second, watching, so silently. The dancer, so changed. Miss Havisham, so vividly present. Puzzled, he runs away again without being sure how the dancer, seated, waiting, there in the dust of another time, is suddenly so transformed. Almost as if she were young again.

*　　　*　　　*

You can go on, says Mercy. Her nose and her throat work together in a strange gesture like a sneer – but more like weariness. It's just an excuse, to say you can't go on. You mean you've had enough. And so what do you want to do about it. Mm? You can't just *stop* going on, you know. Stopping going on is not the opposite of going on. You have to choose somewhere different to go. Go somewhere different. If you really can't go on, prove it. Don't. Do something else instead. What are you going to do – jump out of the window? Just because some child caught you dressed up in some potty old woman's old dress with a great gaping tear down the front? What do you think he saw? What were you doing, tossing yourself off or something? Estella feels quite demystified, and utterly indignant: she had felt the pain and fear of exposure – the violation of it, as she'd felt before the flasher. But both times, the insult directed directly at her. They're in the basement flat. Estella's still in the wedding dress, with a woollen jersey of Mercy's round her shoulders, and they're drinking instant coffee in mugs. (But the world upstairs, the submerged world of the dust and the piano, of Estella at the window where she first saw the dancer's feet posed, scarlet – this the dusty underworld, where real love transposes itself directly from the page of an old story, onto the hearts of women. This world still exists. Why would Mercy deny it? Estella is weary, weary of the contradiction). Mercy's face is bleak from no make-up, but still the shadows and the strong ledges of cheekbone show in her face. Estella has the dark tears of mascara in streaks under her eyes. Streaks of the tapered lines painted by clowns, run downwards from eye to cheek. Symbolic of sadness. There to anticipate the downward lines of the mouth. But in Estella's face, not contrived. An accident of the mascara. Estella's been crying, down in the basement. She feels it's a showdown. She's exposed, playing.

You play too much, Stella, says Mercy. And you read too much. You're very lovable, but you're not of this world. Do you think the rest of us don't love to make faces; to dress up; to play a part? How do you think the rest of us do it? I've got one small mirror in this flat, says Mercy. It's propped on the kitchen window ledge. I use it to put my make up on. When I go to see Andy and be photographed, I dress up before his full length mirror. And that's a rare pleasure. Something to look forward to. It's a luxury. It's a fantasy. What I see there *doesn't exist*, Estella. When I look at you like that I see a silly woman in dressing up clothes. I see you in a heap of some old woman's rags. If you see something else when you look in the glass, then you're fooled. Your reflection *doesn't exist*. It's a figment of your imagination; you're fooled by coherence; duped by synthesis. Go upstairs, says Mercy. Take off those silly old rags. Put them back in the drawer where they belong. Decide what you're going to do. And then do it. While Mercy says all this, makes her speech, something fades out of her face, and Estella hates what she sees. Why should I decide, says Estella, just for the sake of having done with it. That's suicide. Decide what to do and then do it. Do it for ever and never come back. You may be weary, she says to Mercy. You may have found yourself with someone else's life to live. If you wanted to live the life of a baby and distance yourself from the real heart of you, that was your choice. Estella gets up. She's shouting these things, and she picks up a handful of lace to stop herself tripping, with a fluid but forceful movement that means she's angry. She's up, both feet on the ground, and her face is set: a staged anger. She's not here, says the face. Sorry, soft Estella's gone away. I've had it, says Estella. You've had nothing, says Mercy. That's half your trouble. You've had a little uncertainty and a lot of self-induced chaos. You're acting like an old woman, gone senile. You've had nothing, because you haven't made any choices. Look for something outside your wretched mirror. Realise there's a very large framework out there. Take something on. Come on, Stella, says Mercy, softly.

And they go into the hallway, and past a door that's ajar. Look, says Mercy, and, Look. And softly and silently as the night, she tiptoes to the cot where little Mercy is quietly sleeping, curled in a thin, thin shell that keeps her shut out from the choices, for the time being. Furled and cocooned, and Mercy, leaning softly down, puts one finger into the sleeping baby's hand, and the little fist clenches and curls. Look, whispers Mercy. Look, Estella. Touch the little hand. Estella leans down and touches the little curled hand with her index finger, and the tiny fingers softly curl. Mercy opens the little fingers with hers, and gently shows Estella the little pad of softness and warmth, the little soft pad between the fourth and fifth fingers of the baby. Look, says Mercy. Feel the softness. It's like thin, thin velvet. And Estella carefully touches, and the baby stirs in her sleep, then settles again, and Mercy smiles a secret to Estella, smiles a mystery. And kisses the little soft cheek. And they creep softly, softly, sharing some very old secret, out of the room. Estella has, for some reason, to acquiesce.

*　　*　　*

Come on, says Mercy. And they go quickly, quickly; the baby can't be left alone for too long – out of the basement flat, and out into the light. Filtered, out there on the pavement, through the grey-green city leaves of trees, sliding in under the cracked steps: thin sun. Come on, says Mercy, and she's smiling, and she knows. She does know, after all. She smiles with that particular smile: eyebrows levelled, eyes downwards, smiling in spite of a mouth slightly pursed. Estella's busy gathering up the lace in both hands. Trying her best to stop it tangling, to stop it rustling: to stay the chaos of it. Upstairs (looking up at the outside of the house) there's sunlight on dusty curtains. The frail dust of moths' wings; flaked and caked and powdered smooth over the years; the years and years. They're filthy, says Mercy. And then she looks higher up at the house and she smiles the widest and the most secret smile in all the world. Estella follows her gaze. There at the window, the feet are sunning themselves in the trickle of light. Edged with scarlet, and the soles stained brown, resting on the peeling window ledge: stained with dancing for years on dusty floorboards. Ingrained with dust, says Estella. And so must you be, in all those clothes, says Mercy. Estella has again her look of a clear structure; there is a pure synthesis in her face; a pallor, where you would expect shadow. Striking the set. Standing on the bare floorboards, staring out into the pit, into the empty seats. The hollows; the echoes, and the strange ecstasy of the theatre at daybreak. The show's over. A clean break. You need a bath, says Mercy, to Estella.

*　　*　　*

Standing on the bare floorboards of the dancer's upstairs room, to the filtered light of the weakly sun between the old curtains, Estella's alone in the dust, her back to the tarnished mirror, unwinding and unbuttoning and unravelling the wedding dress of old lace, and the dust falls.

Part Six

Do you know what I think about you, says the dancer, sitting forward in her chair at the side of the piano, picking up the dish of chocolates forcefully, presenting it to Estella. Estella smiles and shakes her head. I think you could be a very good writer, says the dancer. Estella wonders if she knows about the wedding dress. She hopes, she prays, she does not. The room is its shrouded self. The dancer is seated, as usual, amongst the debris, and the firm lines of her face have obviously formed, it strikes Estella, watching her from the other side of the room, from her drawing conclusions such as this, in this way, all her life. The dancer's challenging her. Waiting for Estella to ask her why she thinks so. Estella smiles softly back. You have the temperament for it. Says the dancer. You remind me of my mother. She used to write verse, after she left the art school. In the evenings, I can see her now, at her desk. She didn't write anything for ages, then you'd see her at her desk and nothing would distract her. She was gone. My father had to see to the children. You have her look about you, sometimes, I've noticed it quite often. There is triumph of some sort, Estella sees, for the dancer, in this speech.

No, no, she couldn't, says Estella. Ah, but the dancer knows best. But writing's impossible. Says Estella. I'm going to be a painter. Writing's far too complicated. You can only tell stories, that's the problem, if you want any-one to read it. Oh, I don't think anybody read it, says the dancer, back to her usual abstractedness, she never showed it to anybody. I often wonder what happened to it. I would want to say how I felt, says Estella. I wouldn't be able to keep the story moving. I'd want to write a still life. The dancer smiles, at this, as though she thinks Estella's got promise. Estella sees it's no use trying to explain it. She tries, though, since the dancer's in the mood for talking. It's not finding something to say that's difficult, says Estella. In a way, the problem is that you *can't* have something to say, because the writing changes it. She knows this, because of what happened to the painting of Mercy. And you can't stand back, to see if it's working out, like you can when you're painting. There's no sort of edge, between it and you. Painting and dancing are best, says Estella. The dancer smiles in a way that suggests she thinks Estella says this to flatter her. In painting or dancing you start with an idea and you use paint or the body to express it. But in writing, you start with an idea that's in language, and you have to use language to express it in. So you can't get the feel of the edges between what you want to say and the tools you have to say it with. That's the basic problem, says Estella, earnestly. The dancer's having a chocolate. You can't get *between* writing and what you're writing. Says Estella. She refuses a chocolate. But why do you have to? Asks the dancer. You write the idea, and see what comes out.

She feels familiar edges being set up inside her. She wants to cry out, tear a veil. Even just bite a hard chocolate, and feel the dust in her mouth. A feeling of blades and edges, very sharp, yet not sharp enough, shifting like spiders. And yet, a veil of dust over it all, masking it. The feeling makes her face feel red. Anyway. Says the dancer. It sounds to me as though you're a very experienced writer already.

She gathers her skirts and settles them about her. Picking up another chocolate, she strides away. Estella gets up from her chair. She will have to leave, too. Looking back at Estella from the doorway, the dancer has something else to say: the knowing smile still fixed. When you write your novel, she says, I don't care if you put me in it. You can say what you like about me, I don't mind. She turns, she goes.

So that's it. Thinks Estella. She wants me to be a writer because she wants to be in a book. So that she can read it, and find out what she's really like. This shows either a subtle-edged self-knowledge, thinks Estella, or that the dancer is quite mad. After all, she decides, the dancer's probably between the two. All the same, she can hardly believe it. Is it amusing? Is it astounding? Is it conceited? Is it naive? There's really nothing to say, to that. But then, she thinks, it's no stranger than Mercy, wanting to be photographed. Perhaps it's because the dancer's old. Perhaps it's because nobody expects real people to be in novels, anymore. There isn't an answer. But it's a sad and poignant image: the dancer, waiting so patiently and so wryly to see her self in print. Estella tries to remember Mercy, waiting, seated, her arms folded, at the table, framed by the white light, to see the painting of herself. It's no good, she can't work out why it's different. And then she notices, from the inside, that she's smiling the dancer's wry smile.

*   *   *

Estella is sleeping. In her dreams the gypsy has come to save her. She's writing the book about the dancer. He says, leaning over softly to Estella. . . . I will help you write the dancer's story. His slight dark gypsy body would caress her in a second but Estella is made of paper. She flutters in the draughts. A window bangs. The ghost, whispers the dream-voice. Estella and the gypsy – he has ribbons in his hair – labour and paddle in a flood of cider and runny blancmange. Now Estella wears a white dress with a full skirt, white ankle socks and a huge pink bow in her hair. Her cheeks are rouged in circles. The gypsy sits, all coloured with ribbons, at the typewriter. He had told her a story about his mother, who was Japanese. In the night, while he was typing through the hours, the Japanese mother lay awake serenely, and dozed to the sound of raindrops pattering on the roof. She's told him, that now she was getting older, she's noticed that in the dead of night, every night, when the night was most dark, it rained, softly. And all the time it was the pattering keys of the typewriter. And so now Estella composes poems which the gypsy types swiftly onto the typewriter, so that they become real even as Estella says them, softly, to herself. Estella starts to try and make Haiku, which the gypsy knows how to type twice as fast as all other poetry, because it's in his blood. Estella tries one out. She says, In the room the Japanese woman lay listening/Tissue-skin wrapped soft in silk kimono/The sound of raindrops pattered on the roof/She listened in the night./The rain fell softly. Estella tries again, and the gypsy types, little paper fingers, on paper keys, softly, softly. He does not speak. He does not look up. In the room the Japanese woman lay listening/The sound of raindrops pattered on the roof/Far away the gypsy son was typing/The sound of letters pattering in the night/The letters said, My mother broke a plate/A Japanese plate, she said, I am so silly; and Estella runs another poem straight on into the last one, and the cider and runny blancmange mingle around her ankles as she dictates. The gypsy crosses his ankles under his chair behind him, so only his toes get sticky. Estella says, In the dancer's room the girl was eating/The city rocked around her as she paced/The evening closed with little creaks about her/And suddenly she snapped the dark and raced/Uphill to dial a number, when the voice/Responded she could throw away the wrapper.

He sat, still, a little gentle body breathing for the typewriter. One foot in a ballet second position. He worked. Small. She threw books papers remnants of packets and wrappers, threw them down on the bed and as she did so she was changed into a real girl again, with a soft body of flesh, and a scarlet silk skirt and black suede shoes with high stiletto heels. She said, We must go, and buy some food. She said, there is *nothing* in the house. And it was true, the packet of jaffa cakes was empty, and the cider and blancmange pool had quite dried up. So we *must*, said Estella. And it was true, they literally must, and society said they must. Because it was twenty-five minutes to closing time, which somebody else had decided on. And so, indeed, they must. And so forgetting to make poems and leaving the words behind on the typewriter keys in the empty room Estella goes, in her own body, and her own pretty clothes, into the dark, sparkly evening and *rushes* up the hill to the little shimmering shining shop which glimmers like a beacon in the dim road. Like a lighthouse on a little island in the sea. People move brightly in the shop. They wear the costumes and faces of clowns. Their lipstick smiles are cheery. There's a tiny woman in scarlet trousers and she's scented Femme, which Estella recognises – the French mamans wear it. The little woman swops her coins with the harlequins and all Estella's mind is there in the lighthouse, taken up by the harlequins, coloured by their colours. It takes up her body and lets it live. Quick! Estella whispers to the gypsy, quick, open the bag. He opens the big hessian bag he carries in one hand, and he reaches right down to the bottom of it, and pulls out a tiny typewriter. And Estella whispers, so none of the clowns hear her, and her gypsy balances the little typewriter on a corner of the counter. No-one minds, since it's used a lot for balancing purses. Estella whispers and the Japanese friend patters paper fingers and makes a real poem. Estella whispers, In my dream you danced, a harlequin/I was dressed in satin, white, for ballet/When I reached for you there came between us/A huge, dun pantomime horse, and spilling out/Two girls I knew, a wife and a librarian/So everywhere you danced I could not reach you. He puts the typewriter back in the bag and gives the little scarlet woman some coins for it.

When he puts the typewriter back in the bag the lights dim slightly and the harlequins don't have their make-up on any more. Estella is wearing a dull black coat when she next looks down at her body, and holding money in her hand. He slopes, somehow, and carries a small plastic carrier bag. They line up steel cold blocks that will melt into sausages and milk and bananas and mushrooms, all dun and cream and yellow on the little woman's counter and she flashes a steely smile, cold in scarlet. The gypsy is choosing, carefully, two packets of Angel Delight, a strawberry, and a caramel. They pay money into the scarlet woman's hand and Estella feels dirty in black in the brightly-lit shop, the woman shimmering scarlet and the fragrance of Femme. They go out of the shop down the hill, and again into the dark.

It is later, in dream time. The gypsy leans on the bed and it moves. He said I remember the last time I leant on this bed, and it moved. And on the bed the papers were still there. He looked at the clock, and he said, It's time . . . It's time, to go back to work. He rolled up his sleeves. He looked at the sink. She said I'll do that. He rolled down his sleeves. He sat at the typewriter. She poured water and swabbed and scrubbed. She cleaned all the little typed words and all the grease and the sticky brown and pink streaks. And when the little black letters started to collect, from the water, on the plates she was trying to clean, she scooped up a handful and wrapped them up in one of the empty Angel Delight packets. She could enjoy doing all this, because she had to. The room was a heap of papers and washing up, and on the floor where there had been a pool of blancmange and cider, a pool of dry paper was rising. Papers. Papers. Papers, typed the little papery fingers on the delicate papery keys. When she had washed up she cleaned the cooker. She cleaned the sink. She took the little bin of rubbish outside into the dark and emptied it into a bigger, and dirtier bin. She sat. She waited. She paced. It was finished. The Japanese friend was turning away from the typewriter and in his arms, like a bouquet, he held a sheaf of papers, all with small dry words speckled softly over them. It was finished. Estella read all the words and they made no sense. That was not it, at all. Estella was thinking, in a dream voice. He was kneeling on the floor at the foot of the bed. He was leaning over Estella softly, his eyes questioning, sad, and saying, try again, Estella. Do another, Estella, do some more, Estella. But Estella's body was turning to flannel and she could feel Angel Delight rising on the carpet around her ankles.

*   *   *

Estella wakes to the recollection of the dancer's desire to read about herself, and the dream of the strange world of writing, and the gypsy. Perhaps that's the answer, says Estella to herself. The dancer could have a point. She gets up into a sunny morning, and she thinks she'll try to write a poem about the gypsy. The morning dazzles with the new plan. She opens her door softly, so as not to wake the dancer, and she goes downstairs to the faint smell of damsons that always lingers, in the hallway, or in the part of her memory which lodges in the hallway; she clicks open the front door and there's sun on the pavement. The commuters gleam in the sun, hurrying up the hill to the station. Sun on their newspapers, sun filtering through grey serge. Sun in the glint of black patent, sun on the children's hair. And on the step, sun on the milk: two bottles, one for Estella and one for the dancer. Estella shuts the front door. She leaves one bottle just inside the door for the dancer and takes the other upstairs with her, and makes herself milky coffee, in her own French bowl, which she brought back with her from the country there. She sits at the table at the window, and the sun shines on her, she looks out on the amber and the dewy petals and leaves, down on all the lush, auburn colour of it, and feels, here is Estella, there in the room. Her milk in its bowl at her elbow, in the room; she warm in her soft skin, her thighs bare for summer under her red skirt, her eyes, should she regard them in the tarnished mirror on the other side of the room, pale and light in the fine, blonde face. Bright, for the possibilities still left at this, an early hour.

There's a small nagging, dragging wrench, though. Something amiss in the deep, deep heart of Estella. Something, a little flutter which, were Estella to home in on it, to settle herself around the presence of it, to softly, quietly, touch it with her fingertips, something which would need a scream and a wrench, a backward fling from Estella's body, a blow in the stomach, or a cut, a neat, fatal slice, to silence it. Something, on the other side of Estella. But to deal with it Estella would need a different body. There's no doubt about it. And Estella's already checked the mirror today, and decided it's all right: she'll accomodate this image: a natural, dewy, finely drawn Estella. Sunny Estella, all fine lines and sunlight on the dew, the early morning Estella. And so Estella turns her back on her image, and sits at the table, now her writing desk. Today's the first day of a new structure. She will stop eating chocolate and her stomach will discipline itself to the fine lines of the dance. So organised, Estella will write . . . she picks a sheet, her thinnest sheet, of paper, and rolls and furls it into the typewriter and thinks of some words to be the images of the deeply concealed secrets of women. Such words as might be suggested by the particular veiled and literary mystery set up by the creation of her own namesake. Estella.

* * *

Once, Estella loved a gypsy, she writes on the page. But then, the truth of what she told the dancer starts to intrude. She cannot write what she means. Once Estella loved a gypsy: she tries again. The day she was upset, the gypsy leaned over her to comfort her. His dark gypsy body would caress her at any moment, but there is a reason why he can't. It's all started so badly, thinks Estella, reading it over, that she will let her imagination run away with her, and stop trying to keep things in check. If it smacks of madness, so much the worse. Tant pis. And so, she goes on. Estella and the gypsy – he has ribbons in his hair – flounder together in a flood of cider and runny blancmange. Estella wears a white dress with a full, stiff skirt, white ankle socks and a large pink bow in her hair. Her cheeks are rouged in circles of powdered scarlet. The gypsy sits, his ribbons gleaming, at the typewriter. He tells her a story about his gypsy mother. In the night she lay awake on her mat and listened to the sounds of raindrops pattering on the roof. Little did she know, though, that it was the gypsy, typing. Estella sits at her table in the early, dewy light, and writes her dreams.

Part Seven

Estella and Mercy meet in the city, for an evening, to treat themselves. They dress up for the occasion; they eat in a restaurant. They have candles and low lighting and a bottle of wine, just like the couples around them at the other tables. The other couples are there to mingle gender in the candlelight, unlike Estella and Mercy. Leaning towards each other, into the space in the middle of the table, with the candle as its focus. Looking for a secret there, seeking a mystery. Estella watches them do it. But Estella and Mercy too, in their way, are there for romancing. They both love the sparkle of the wine, and the candlelight, and the way the lighting sets everything dazzling to the smell of Indian food. They are there to luxuriate in this too. It makes me feel guilty, somehow, says Estella, to be eating in a restaurant without a man – it feels very extravagant when I'm not paying for the sex of it. It doesn't make me feel guilty at all, says Mercy. Mercy, Estella sees, refuses to see; so Estella resists. And so, Mercy: leaning across a dingy red restaurant table cloth her neck pale where her white cotton blouse is open. She wears a white blouse with a little collar and a tweed jacket: Mercy, uncharacteristically restrained. She wears three plain gold and three plain silver rings on her fingers. She wants more wine, after they have drunk one bottle, but doesn't buy it because she doesn't have enough money. Estella thinks of the other Mercy, Mercy in silver lurex, her legs and hair scarlet and her eyelids sparkling silver. Receiving a twist of silver from the gypsy. Thinks of her painting the city red, thinks of her in Clive's apartment, eating piece after piece of salami, spoonful after spoonful of creamy mayonnaise and pink taramasalata. The free spirit Mercy; Mercy, the child of the Tempest. Tonight there is a refusal about her. Something sealed in. It is as though her colours have been dimmed by the candlelight.

She's in a strange mood tonight, Mercy. She says, I remember you on your first day at the dancer's, Estella. You were so melancholy, you were like an Autumn leaf falling. I wasn't melancholy, says Estella, I was selective. I was choosing which way I would see things. But it's true: she feels Autumn leaves falling all about her, over the table, in the restaurant; dappled by the low lighting and the odour of curry. Mercy's ear-rings glimmer a little gleam of something silver in the fading, sepia light of Estella's first day at the dancer's house. The restaurant could be lined with trees and dappled with brown leaves: Mercy is so bland tonight, in her tweed jacket, and Estella feels there is so much between this table and her first day at the dancer's house. And yet, so little. She notices that the tiny hole for Mercy's ear-rings is made at the very bottom of the lobe, and off-centre, which makes the slivers of silver hang lackadaisical, loopy, eccentric. Estella wonders if this is meant. And, did the gypsy pierce Mercy's ears for her? She hopes he did – there would be a kind of poetic justice in this. With his syringe. His silver machine. This is very likely, Estella hopes he did. It would be fitting. Mercy is translucent in the silver light. Like a mermaid, Estella thinks, though the blouse is wrong for that. Her hair is full and bright and loose and her skin is fine and brown in the open-necked, cool white blouse: glimpses of bone and shadow, in the half-light. Estella hopes her skin is fine and brown, and that her bones make shadows in the candle light.

*   *   *

Now what is the matter with Estella tonight? asks the fine brown Mercy. You seem very edgy, she says, sending up wisps of smoke between herself and her slim brown cigar. I'm just thinking, says Estella. Just thinking about being here. Looking at the spaces on the other tables, and wondering what's in them, what the couples see, to make them all lean into them in that way. I feel ashamed of being a girl on her own, Estella says, to Mercy. I feel ashamed and guilty about it. People think there's something wrong with you. Think of the fun of arriving at parties, bringing that space in the middle of the table with you. The joy of arriving with someone, – and having enough colour and enough space for both of you, reflected back on you. People look towards you and see something so much bigger and so much brighter. But then, I think of my space in the dancer's room. There, the space is filled with all my own props. Everything means something – something to do with either things I hope for, or things I remember. Everything's to scale. Scaled to me, and my dreams. I pull out drawers, I look in cupboards. And everything in there has a purpose. Because nothing got there unless I put it there. And if I think of a man on the bed, the room changes. The perfume changes, its essence of France and paintings is absent. And it can't get its perspective. Its continuity is all broken up. I like my own continuous, consistent space. Unbroken. There I can walk and dance and think at my own pace. Without anyone getting it wrong.

I know what you mean, says Mercy coolly. But it can't last, Estella. You'll tire of it. You're tired of it already. It's getting on your nerves. You ought to let go a bit, Estella. But I have let go! says Estella. That's the whole point of being at the dancer's house. That's the whole *point*. If it's the whole *point*, says Mercy, you haven't let go.

I feel like a puppet, says Estella, the wine in her breasts and eyelids. I feel painted and smooth, like a puppet, but with no-one pulling my strings. What I notice, she says, – smartly, she feels – about men, is that they pull the strings to put themselves in the picture. They come onstage masked in black, with black gloves, all sombre, like commuters, but all the same – so visible, everyone has to look at them and realise they're in charge. Because the audience likes to watch the process; the mechanics of it, not just the show. The technics are as enthralling, for them, as the dancing. They like to see the whole process enacted. And the man who pulls the strings – the choreographer, the executioner, is himself a figure in the tableau. Without him, the dance is meaningless. The puppet is the curio, the centre-piece, but it's the man in black who's really the impulse of the dance. Mercy smokes, and looks, and listens.

Estella's getting earnest with the wine: It's all too easy, she says, to marry the choreographer. The one in black who pulls the strings. It makes you look more forceful. Your dancing takes on a structure. People think they see why you're there. It's all too easy to be the puppet. But you want to be the puppet, says Mercy entering into the spirit of things. You like the way puppets look. You should be the little glossy, painted doll. You'd adore it, Estella. It would make you feel beautiful. And you would fall in love with the choreographer and never leave him. It's exactly as you say, says Mercy, leaning her elbows on the table, balancing her fingers and her cigar, all laced together, like a rose on a stem. You'd love it. Because it's exactly as you say – except that there's no-one watching.

* * *

Estella and Mercy leave the restaurant. Mercy collects her things together. Lighter, cigars, bag, keys. She says, what a lot of things. They ride in a bus in the late evening. Through the windows: houses with crumbling steps up to high front doors; rows of greying net curtains; two big peeling posters for two glasses of lurid yellow advocat, side by side. Dusty lorries slouching in the kerbs. Cold, black, living streets, grimy with the dust of trying. Every day. Cold, black, asleep streets. The park: its trees still and massed in the dark. One squat little bird, Estella has seen, walking in the park at this time of night. Breathing silently and alone on a path. Breathing softly in the night.

They creep quietly down the basement steps and it's still

and quiet down there. The house is dark except for one little dim light, where the neighbour waits, minding the baby, for Mercy to return. She leaves the house quietly, stealthily: not to wake the baby Mercy. Estella goes into the dim room with the faded green sofa and the baby's things strewn. Mercy goes to look at the baby. Estella is very sleepy with wine. She rests her head on the arm of the faded green sofa and feels her eyes closing. In the hallucinatory no-man's land between sleep and waking where red wine wafts its shadows and illumines the walls of the mind with images, here Estella has a dream. Mercy is a woman and Estella is a little girl, dressed in white broderie anglaise with sleeves just to her elbows. They're having a conversation in a restaurant, by candle light, but then the scene changes. It's all a field dappled with faded poppies. The field and Estella and Mercy are all veering down a slope and you know that at the top of the slope there is a line of houses, with their lights on. Estella and Mercy cascade down the slope rouged with poppies, waterfalls of women, and Mercy has her hair piled in a luxurious but tumbling chignon. She wears a black skirt which hangs in folds to her ankles, tight at the waist in a belt clasped with a brooch of silver. The white blouse is high at the neck, it has a stand-up colour. She says, into the air, where Estella is falling, falling down the slope among the poppies: What about Monsieur Satie? Her voice has an echo. Oh, you loved him *so* much, echoes the voice of Mercy. Why didn't you marry him? whispers the voice. Estella. Estella? choruses the echo in the poppies. Estella's falling, falling: All that terrible solitude, she shouts up at Mercy, who has regained her balance and is walking gracefully through the field of poppies, which at her level is on flat ground. All those murderous bare rooms, shouts Estella, all those dusty floorboards, all those peeling walls. The old, old oak cupboards all full of the same black dress suit, eleven replicas, and he wearing the twelfth his whole lifetime because he was so absent-minded. But he loved you! trails the voice of Mercy, down the slope. She is still walking, and smiling. Go back! shouts

Mercy. Knock on Monsieur Satie's door and he will play you a tune. Ask him to pick a new one out for you. He'll write you a new composition HE WILL PULL YOUR STRINGS, sings the voice. Why not? Why not? sounds the echo of Mercy's voice, in the poppies. But Estella's already at the bottom. Everything speeds up. She's a sleek and scarlet cat. She purrs. Thin, separate, resonant sounds. Reedy, fluted sounds. A mouth breathing thin notes into a flute. I am substance, says Estella the cat to herself. I am woman. She smiles, at this, because she knows she is really a cat. I will curl on my very own carpet of scarlet. But the carpet she curls on is moving: it is not solid. It was only the lighting that made it seem so. It is an indigo pit, made only of shadow. Estella gasps, and Mercy, from the top of the slope, now far away, calls an ominous warning: Estella! Estella! says Mercy, wobbling the sofa beneath Estella. Estella! Wake up and drink some coffee. You were snoring like an old dog. Oh, Estella.

* * *

Oh, Mercy, says Estella. I had such a strange and eccentric dream. I dreamt of Eric Satie. And then I woke to thoughts of a person who keeps coming in disguise into my dreams and haunting me. This is it. Estella must tell Mercy about the gypsy. She must confess. The wine will speak his name. She feels as though he is watching her. Someone is always watching. And the one, of course, who watched Mercy and the gypsy, is Estella. She must tell Mercy, and make her realise about the silent audience. It is because Mercy doesn't know how Estella used to watch them, that the gypsy haunts Estella. But there is a worse thing and this thought makes a sensation like something falling, deep in the pit of her. There is the card she wrote the gypsy. It's that which is giving her strange dreams and making her feel the sensation of falling as she wakes. The card she wrote to the gypsy, so that he would come to the dancer's house. Even as she did this, she knew it was wrong.

She told him a little story of the dancer's house. Now he knows he can come there. As long as Estella is sitting on the stairs, or sunning herself on the steps of the powdery outside, or watching the Autumn – hoping to see in it the approach of the gypsy – through the dancer's window, then, the gypsy will run up the steps, his eyes on Estella's slim and brown ankles, his fingers caressing the hem of her skirt as she runs up the steps in front of him. Into the cool, into the dim, into the powdery house. And then Mercy will not see him. After Estella posted the card she had planned to wait at the window, or on the steps, until he came. She would see him coming up the street. But what if Mercy, looking out-and-upwards through the basement window, recognised his shoes on the steps. They were distinctive shoes. Good ones: though old now, black leather, with laces. What if Mercy and the baby were outside in the sunshine, and they saw the gypsy running up the road to meet Estella – and thought he meant them. What if the gypsy made a mistake – indeed, this was quite likely – and went down to the basement, expecting to see Estella, and found Mercy and the baby Mercy instead. Then, Mercy would know that Estella had sent for him. She must tell Mercy what she has done. And this means telling her that when the gypsy ran in from the outside to the pub with the red flocked wallpaper, and reached for the twist of silver paper, and slid it between Mercy's fingers,: they had a silent audience. Estella. And there could be no reason for her watching, that she can think of, except that she watched them because she wanted to be them. This is what makes Estella so ashamed.

And there is another problem to do with telling Mercy about the gypsy: not that Estella had sent him a card, not that she had watched him, wait for Mercy. This is a more superstitious reason. It is as though if she shattered the image of the gypsy by telling Mercy, then the spell would be broken. Speaking the gypsy's name somehow threatened the credibility of Mercy and the dancer, and the dancer's house. The gypsy must be kept a secret, to keep the whole web of events, and the setting, and

Mercy and the dancer – to keep them tenable. That was somehow the key to a mystery: keeping the silence of the gypsy's name. And yet, Estella had written the card to the gypsy. That could only be because she wanted to be forced to break the spell, and see what happened. Because telling the secret about the gypsy would give her access to a knowledge which would make her, Estella, more credible.

Once I was in love, says Estella. Mercy has acknowledged her drunkenness with black coffee, so it's O.K. for her to begin this way. The wine colours everything translucent red. I was in love with a man I didn't know. I loved him from afar. Do you think that's possible? I thought he was a gypsy because I always wanted to love a gypsy and he seemed somehow unconnected to things in the way that gypsies are. He wasn't really a gypsy, though. He would slip twists of silver paper to people who slipped him ten pound and twenty pound notes – all very quickly – the whole exchange in a second. I said to myself, with the money he will buy ribbons for a gypsy woman's hair, and muslin dresses for a little gypsy baby. The gypsy woman would be waiting for him on the steps of the caravan, nursing the baby, her skirts spread wide. Is it possible to love from afar?

Mercy smiles, she nods her head.

He wasn't really a gypsy, says Estella, he wore a shirt of small checks, and carried a newspaper. His shoes were good. They were black leather, with laces. Estella watches Mercy, who frowns a little, concentrating, rather than guessing.

He had one glass eye, says Estella.

Mercy looks up. Quickly.

What happened? She rapped in a strange way, it out.

If I'm right, says Estella, she picks up a cushion, she plays with its tassels, she keeps her eyes down, she plaits the tassel. She looks up at Mercy. She says, He loved you.

Mercy raises her eyebrows with no movement of the rest of her body or her face. She surveys Estella long and cold. Hard, and cold. What are you talking about. She says. What the hell do you mean. Are you quite mad? Or are you just irresponsible. I really didn't know him, says Estella. I used to say hello and he used to smile at me and we pretended we knew each other it was a kind of game. The ridiculous thing is – the thing I know was very stupid – I found out where he lived. I sent him a card and it had this address on. I mean, my address, of my room upstairs. But it's the same address, she says weakly.

Well you can sleep in your bed tonight, says Mercy. He's dead. She gets up and, literally, shows Estella out. Like a bank manager.

So the gypsy wasn't coming.

Part Eight

When Estella woke up in the warm, sickening morning she decided to start again. This was the day she decided, really in her mind, to go back. Going back was looking in the mirror and seeing the real, pale canvas of Estella. There were so many women in the world, all painted different colours and dressed in different ways – so that you knew which was which – and you chose. And you were, having chosen, that woman. Estella had been three women. That was the difficulty. She had been the beautiful, the delicate French maman. Stilettos and St. Laurent. Smelling poignantly of a perfume special to money; nails manicured; sipping China tea, and shopping for furniture. And then she had been the amber-haired woman, leaning on the area steps, jewelled and tarty, inside a room of tapestries and feathers; old clothes and paintings; the cheap and the nasty; and the oh, so exotic. And, she had been the waiting and the painting Estella. The Estella whose knees and whose shoulders were so boney, whose hip bones were so like birds' wings, who dressed so black, who ate so little and drank so much, that she, from her frail pedestal of control, could fashion and mould and sculpt a whole image of a painted self, out there in the distance. The old Estella bought cracked pottery and dull jewels and old paintings and books with photos of Colette and Sarah Bernhardt. The old Estella read the stories of the Nineties. And the old Estella lived, so decked out and so painted and so surrounded, as to be modelled by the clutter and the jewels which surrounded her. In the old days, Estella collected the accessories, and, adorning and surrounding herself with these, modelled, within, as she walked and looked and read, a real image of Estella. So that looking in the mirror she saw a moulded, a sculpted form, a shape, and that, the sculpted image, was Estella.

Estella wakes from formless dreams of the gypsy's quick presence, dreams which circled around, in the centre of her mind, an absence – a space unfilled by any form that might represent Estella. Or the gypsy. Estella, waking from such dreams, knows now, that it's no good. She can do nothing without a make-believe beginning. Something must take place. She can tolerate no more of those surfaces, and the emptiness beneath them. No good, without a model; without an image, to represent herself. Going on without knowing the shape you want to make, makes energy released into nowhere. Energy without reflection. It's, starting from nowhere. Estella knows, waking in the dull morning, from dreams of confusion, knows she can't exist without a finished form, a clear image of herself, to represent. It's all a painting. Or it's never started. Man can do nothing, endorses Estella to herself, safe in her world of painted images, without the make-believe of a beginning. Nor can we, she says to herself. Ha ha, thinks Estella. Good.

The dancer is getting up. She's pacing and bathing and making tea and there's an aroma of toast and Estella knows she will never again eat toast. One day soon, Estella will be thin again. Thin as a statue, thin as a thread of paint on a canvas, and thin as the models in the glossy magazines. For the time being, Estella will act as though she is thin, and the game can begin again. Can take place. Estella gets up, to the slam of the front door after the dancer and she puts on Frank Zappa and she dances to the bursting and the falling apart, the ripping open of the music. She dances to the upsurging strokes of the brush on the canvas, and she's light on her feet. And she knows it's time for a new start. What will she wear, to travel the memory? How will she look, to get back in the part?

Estella pulls down a hanger, and it's heavy with taffeta. The pleated skirt swivels and falls. She puts it on, – prepares for a new gypsy. In dramatic black, or red. There is no other kind of preparation. Red, scarlet red. Estella swirls in scarlet red taffeta now and she's got black stockings and she's got bright deep scarlet leather shoes.

Red shoes. Estella swirls taffeta. There in the room next to the dancer's; there in her own pretend theatre. The theatre of her imagination. Swirls it and caresses it in her hand; and, in the mirror, sees scarlet tips of fingers. And unfurls and peels the black stockings, and instead slides tights for dancing and hard, tapered thighs – stockings are for bed; and a vulva of musk; frayed silk; the spider – and looks at herself. She swirls in the room; and, in the mirror, the image of a scarlet Estella swirls in a duller, tarnished room. Or just a part of it. Only a part of it; a slice or a fragment. A smithereen. Some black specks of dust. All that part of the room is filled with Estella and only Estella. There's nothing else to be seen: it's too much red. When Estella undoes it at the waist the taffeta skirt slithers and slumps and slides to the ground. A doll, fallen forward at the jointed waist.

Nothing is happening. There is a space, somewhere, between Estella and an unnamed, wider vista. Some raised platform between Estella's body and her mind which she cannot mount. The step up to it is too steep. And yet, she knows that this would be only the first step – the first step, or a doorway: a threshold to a broader, a less constricted world. She cannot take it. At the top of the steps, a small platform, from which, a view: padded streets: black on sparkling black of them, dazzling in the rain. Looking down on them, you are trapped between their walls.

Estella puts the skirt on the bed; drapes it. And finds a new colour. She picks pale pink tights for dancing and she finds black patent ballerina pumps like glossy dancing shoes. And she stretches and spreads her legs: one on the floor, straight and strong, for balance; the other, taut, moving in a slow arc. A broad, wide sweep of a line; a thin, tapering sweep of a line, encircling her body in a thin arc. And it's a dancing day; a day for disco music. And she dances, stretching to her own hummed music, her own Diaghilev. She's poised and she's strong and she's out there and she's special. She rushes and flicks through the clothes on the rail and she finds something powder blue and fitted: tight on shoulders, slender at the waist; and she stretches and dances and in the mirror are reflected a myriad mirrors: a veritable maze of mirrors. Other rooms surround her: other places, with other possibilities. Other spaces, to run and dance in, and so Estella tips Chanel 19 and dusts the little sprinkles around her neck and shoulders. She lifts down the mirror and she sees tapered, shapely ankles: strong, shapely bones she sees; and the hard calves of dancers, and the bones of her knees like rings on her fingers: a clearly defined, a shapely adornment. Added, on purpose, to enhance. And so, she's pastel. Pastel for light-headed; pastel for Spring; for nymphets, and juke box music; a mixture: plastic and pastoral: ice creams in the country-side. Pale blues and pinks, for the late, warm afternoon, and a new awakening.

And so, Pale blue and pale white and pale yellowy blonde Estella's Miranda, waking on the island. Impish and daring; provocative, and ready for fun. Those are pearls. Those are pearls threaded in her hair. But it's just the light, filtered through blonde. Sunlight through a filigree of pearls and lace. Light on the sunny hair. Over the railway bridge.

Over the railway bridge, and onto the train, and then she's reading the titles on the juke box. There's something – a frenzied feeling – pushing through her and inside her and to the music. Drawing her in, yet still setting her apart. Apricots, just ripening. All the fullness of mellow fruit; pale down. The white wine's darkening clearly all through her body. The winey water sparkles in the glass. White for the night; and for the feeling. And everyone around her is big in woollen sweaters. They haven't shaved, and one's starting a fight with another. Or they're lolling, dull-eyed, on cardboard boxes or plastic tables, for seats. And it's all dirt: all the black and smutty kind of dirt that is none of your (Estella's) business. It's not part of you and it wasn't you who made it so dirty; you couldn't. And so it stays right outside the space which is you. So you don't mind being among it. A colour for the others. Like so much that makes people like Estella and the dancer as they are. Erect (or cocooned) on their own island; in their own space. How do you be, in the black dirt that is other people's spaces. What do you do? Black dirt; all sport; being naked with children; talking about Insurance. Estella and the dancer aren't insured. What do you do? How do you live, in the wrong space, even for half an hour, or a few moments? Some men get the guide book, so they know their way around, and they just go in there and somehow stay intact. Because they know it's allowed and it's possible, it's even within their rights. And because it's within their rights they're all right in there, and they can stay there and even relax. But women like Estella and the dancer disappear. They negate themselves, not wanting to be there, feeling that though it's authorised it isn't somehow, substantiated. And so they negate themselves, so there's just a body, in the wrong space. But even the body (the woman looks down; surveys herself) is changing shape: it's expanding and expanding. There's a double chin (the woman peers down) and it's too thick round the waist. The eyes are dull and have no expression and don't reflect the light of the woman looking down on the dull image. And so you can't control it. And if you can't, you can't. It's all too late. Clearly. And that's when they let them eat cake. And that, if they eat it often enough, late enough, proves it. So don't get in the wrong space. Better to be selfish. Better to be irredeemably solipsistic. Better to phase out; fade out; remain anonymous. But that's eccentricity.

There's a sinking, a woozy sensation, lots of little nerves dying glamorously, in Estella's body. Running all over and inside it. They're all curling back, every nerve, curling and dying, like miniature dying swans, thin as the legs of spiders, keeling over, curling up. Estella's in love. Something's coming, she can tell, she's poised on the brink of it. There's a Christmas Eve anticipation in the atmosphere tonight. This must be how

Romance begins. And, sure enough, there at her side, there is a stranger. A man in black who smiles a lopsided smile which is the gesture of a promise, to Estella. It could all begin here, now, between Estella and this silent one.

Estella's poised and vivid in her own space and tentatively, suggestively at the edge of it; at the very precipice, she says something and when he smiles nothing breaks the surface of his face. Estella responds, to what he says: she says something herself. They sit down. What do they talk about? About the others, and the movies, the others again. Oh, you know, just what a lady should. (And Estella says she feels alone, and she feels full of wine, and that she's dancing inside. There's a leaping in her.) And around those things she mentions other things; things from another space; a space somewhere apart; it's one they both enter together, and, ranged round the space, the boulders, and, a little to the right of the canvas, a pale little blurred streak. An Impressionist's blur; pale pink and moving. Estella. And that's the space they talk about. Voices over. The real confrontation goes on in an underworld of contact; a strange current; in a new space, which they create as they go. A gleaming, a tense edge. A thin line between their bodies; and they're both walking it. Estella feels that line in her mouth and in her breast, like a thin thread through her body; a series of threads; a series of spider's legs. Nerves on a knife edge. Making a cutting edge as they curl,. woozy outwards and backwards and inside out of themselves. And so their fingers touch, or, Estella's fingers touch the man's. And he takes her hand and so touches, all at once, every little nerve thread simultaneously. Setting up all the little vibrations, which simmer to the centre, and by brushing, thus, the tips of her fingers, he touches the core of that spider that is Estella. They're on the train and then out in the strange dark. It's not the same brink of space any more: no more cocooned in the light. He's walking by the side of her, on a strange platform; in a strange place. And she's walking by the side of him. It's her old space, but inside her the spider legs are stretching; pulling something taut in her chest and in her throat. A spider's web, and some insect hooked by one thin antenna. Estella's hooked and she links his arm as they walk down the quiet, night street into a special atmosphere of cold, acrylic stillness. An atmosphere for a new street; for strangeness, for a new awakening. Walking together, hearing both their footsteps, and it's this house here and in the hallway a tiny black kitten. Black coffee, and the brown leather sofa: the comfort of wear in its deep seat, and Estella's tired and so she's led up the stairs to the big bed. Big enough for two, as they usually are. Not Estella, though. Usually. Estella has a beautiful body, and he says O, Estella, you are very beautiful. This must be the start, Estella thinks. This is the start of something that will last my whole life. I will fold babies to my breast in this bed (or one a lot like it) and you will always be there by my side to say how beautiful I am. This is it, thinks Estella.

In the morning it's a new life. Estella's been awake all night holding the man close to her, smelling a new special smell, breathing a new life. The world is spinning. There's a dizzy sunlight, on frost. A new morning. A new dawning, and it's warm in the very centre of Estella. Weirdly, Estella will have babies in this bed. Strangely, Estella's body is a body for having babies, a body to bear new lives. And that's because the life here, in this room, after the night, in this strange sunlight, is too much to bear. Her body will break if it goes on beating like this. Estella will never write, never read, never paint again. She will run and run in the sunlight and she will wallow in waves of her own nerve ends, stretched on the floor singing poetry she already has the words to in her body. . . .

She will play the Gymnopédies and one Brahms Intermezzo and one little section of the Pathétique on her piano, all her life. Nothing will change, her body cannot support a single thing that is new, after this night. (The man is still sleeping). She has arrived, and everything for ever more will be a celebration of what she has contained in her body. So to make new life, to move forwards, she will have a new Estella. A brand new tiny and curling small soft Estella, whose hair will be black and whose eyes will be blue and who will dance for all her life in a theatre with a red plush curtain. And Estella will be there in a red dress. In her body, this time, not just in her head, or in her dreams. And the man wakes up and he sees Estella and tells her she is beautiful and then downstairs puts apples and yoghurt on a tray, saying she's not obliged to go, she can stay. But Estella must go, she must go away and be the new Estella he has made of her. She must hurry and run on light feet with her hair in a tangle and her eyes (she will look in the mirror as soon as she is home) will be so much more sparkling and more glittering than she has ever seen them and truly she will be, from now on, a beautiful woman, made so by a man who looks good beside her because he is beautiful too. And later Estella looks, and she sees Estella, but Estella so transformed and so radiant and so sparkling and vivid and fine boned and so, oh so – translucent – that she is overwhelmed by what she has become, overnight, and knew it was always meant to be this way, and that she can have babies now and there will be tiny warm bodies at her breast and she knew she deserved it and the time has come, at last.

*   *   *

In the morning the street outside is crisp and very cold, and the glare of day, after this night, is unreal. The world's unreal: it belongs to other people. It's Gerald Crich's street, the one he walked in after his night in the small, dank, unfamiliar house. Gudrun waving in the doorway. Estella feels like Gudrun in the doorway, her face wan with a new test. But she's also Gerald Crich: her shoes too loud and too clipped on the paving stones; strange to herself, after a new beginning. And a pale sky. Though bright, with a stark paleness that reflects the new and giddy transparency in Estella. The park in the dream of morning is all drizzle on frost. Estella's body warms to the coldness of a thin mist, though no thin pin striped shafts of fine cold can pierce her last night's skin. He is tanned and of bronze, and only this bronze can penetrate the pale skin of Estella. He is bronzed and firm and sculpted and so beautiful. He holds Estella close to him and she, smaller and slighter and finer, fits and yearns. They fold like petals, really, and he says you are so beautiful. So beautiful. So beautiful. Oh you are so *gorgeous*. Estella's tender and slight and is it the mist or is it he who envelops her? How can I make all this hard and thin, asks Estella, a sheet of metal to pin to my wall. A butterfly, turned to paper and preserved for ever in the form it died in. A slither, a slice, of the stark, fine light, the fine lines and breaths of this night, to keep forever, on a page. Fine and precious as paper. How can I preserve this feeling? If she can find a way, it might last forever. I wish you could stay says Estella in the air, in the morning, in her tiredness. I wish you could stay. And she smiles up at him, releases a gesture, and hopes it will reach him, a smile for him in their same early morning; and knows he'll never know about the spaces between them.

* * *

Such a hot day she can't breathe so, in dark colours, navy and scarlet, she sits on the front steps leans against the rusty railing the sun's scorching her skirts trailing her calves and, just so hot, she's sketching on thin white paper. So hot she can't breathe, and she looks down the road for the new lover who will come, instead of the gypsy. She won't come too, because she's here on the steps already and so far away, her dancing legs triangular. She tests the base of her spine against the steps, in the heat. Her feet are bare and there are two lines of Estella. One in the triangle of her legs and one in the straight line of her spine. Planes in relation: Estella's posed to be sculpted. She looks along the road. She's the gypsy's wife, she can't help it, her skirts spread, sitting on the steps of the vivid caravan. She shields her eyes, dark in the heat, with her slim finger bones. Her hands are ringed and her feet are bare and hot on the flaking stone of the steps. The cold stone is boiling hot. Dust hot. Just so hot it is stifled and smothered and unbreathing in the heat. The stone will surely crack. Nothing moves. The sun in her eyes. Navy and scarlet spread patches of dark like blood on the flaking stone.

*   *   *

Inside the house, cool on the staircase she sits, shaded but still now stifled by her own heat. Nude ankles on high heels, she sits, trailing her feet. Waiting for him to come, all the long afternoon. And when he comes he's running, still in the acres and acres he ran to get here, still running in those spaces, large and outside, somewhere, there in the little room. Elsewhere. Turning, slightly, angular, as though measuring his weight on the frail floor. Standing, to drink. His thighs are hard in the room where her ankles are frail and taut and thin boned on thin heels. She is weak with the heat and so she reclines, she folds, she crumples, she stretches, limply. He crosses the room. They turn and fold and whichever shape they make she's always hidden and secreted within him: inside his body, gathered up. Estella feels, always a yearning, as though she's somewhere else, always a reminder that he takes up more of the space, drinks in more of the sunlight, than she, and that when he leaves her it's as if he flips, simply, in a somersault, to arrive, the joker, at the feet of somebody else: a dark-haired woman. Turning up; breathing hard from the jump, but smiling his lopsided smile, pat he comes. Off he goes. It's not love if you don't come with me, he says, but Estella can't. She's trapped in the room, waiting for him.

And when he's gone she comes back. Slowly, lithe on the floor, bending one knee over the other stretched leg, reaching for a book; a drink, waiting, in gypsy colours, navy and scarlet, for the time, stretched out on a knife edge. The day is too hot, and she is dressed too darkly. Fair as she is, the heat is too heavy. Breathing gently she's waiting again in a single space, in a single room, coming and going, shadowy in a corner, arranging her dancer's legs, waiting for a break.

*   *   *

You fell in love with him, says Mercy. You fell in love with him! That's what you did, you fell head over heels, like the joker; the fool; the jester, and that's what's happening and that's why you're here in this room and that's why you feel dizzy and that's why you want to dance and why you put on black baggy trousers and dancing shoes and ran to the hairdresser to get your Cinderella hair neatened and preened. And that, says Mercy, is why you're so happy all suddenly, about being alone. The space around you has widened, and in your image of you he's there walking beside you and there's a sparkle in your eyes. And where is he? Estella thinks he'll tell *her*. This week-end. He'll go to her and say look, I'm sorry. You're good enough for real life but now I've found make-believe. A Miranda. A special, unique and pearly person in a new space, on a new island. And I'm sorry, I know you can drive a car and sign a contract and take a plane to offices the world over, but I've found someone now who speaks a new language and who lives in a room in a dancer's house and who wears old taffeta and who can walk right out of the space of the real world and find a new space, with a stage, to love in; to love on. I will relinquish your fortune, your success, he will say. For the luxury of lace and pearls, for the feel of soft silk on my skin and on her skin. I will go with her into the wings and find grease paint and faded costumes, into a world where there is no money but where there is art. I have been wrong, he will say. Forgive me, I have made a mistake. I have chosen the wrong space and I must leave you. . . . Along such lines as these; words to that effect. And this is why she is happy and dancing and making spaghetti bolognese with lots of garlic in a big pot on the Baby Belling. Stirring and tipping more wine.

*   *   *

Dark in the room, as the light changes colour, makes the room gloomy. Estella and Mercy have by now drunk too much of the wine and eaten too much of the spaghetti and Mercy in shadow there in the smoke of her own cigarette, takes discomfort in this dizzied attempt by Estella to make a blur and a streak of the uncomfortable space left behind by the man who is out there in the world driving and eating in restaurants and dancing in discos with his rightful counterpart. He is not in this room therefore he is elsewhere. That's Mercy's reasoning. Mercy believes always in the hard fact. Something hard to hold in your hand. It has matter, therefore it exists. And any desire or any amount of yearning, even, any lush imagining, is not, in Mercy's view, the actuality. And has a decent chance of not materialising. But she doesn't tell Estella. After all, Estella is so warm, and so soft, that Estella might be able to exert influence; work magic. There are women who can, Mercy has heard. Though not in her experience. I have to go, Stella, says Mercy, it's getting late and it's getting colder. You should go to bed and have sweet dreams. And Estella says she will, and picks up sticky white pieces of spaghetti and wraps them carefully in a piece of paper, which she folds and puts in the little basket. And there she is at midnight, washing dirty dishes, drinking the last of the wine from the bottle, still in her dancing shoes. She smooths and rubs enormous bowls and pans, dries fine glasses, and stacks the things neatly in the little cupboard for one. But, two of everything, tonight. And she's glowing and she's happy and she's excited, still, about the cold, grey morning which she feels still in her body. And deep in the night she's turning in her bed, a little restlessly, because too much wine has made of her mind a blankness, which her body tightens and turns to try and obliterate.

*   *   *

It is a long hot Sunday – as long as five o'clock she's waited. The time in the afternoon when, if it's not happened yet, you can't make it happen now and you can even stop worrying about it: it becomes, at five o'clock, a day like other people's days and you can sit back now in the late afternoon and watch them: that's all you have to do to be like them. And so, in the hot afternoon, all prepared in navy and high black stiletto heels teetering in bare legs, her nails scarlet, her neck and hair all deep in Chanel 19, Estella opens the digestives and she slices a sliver of cheese. She gets the white wine out of the fridge and she selects one glass and there's a knock on the door and she hadn't known. He had been coming up the steps and she hadn't known and there he was. He is under this roof! She mis-quotes, and smiles. He is under this roof and he's in her arms everywhere in the room and the sunlight's dizzying and dazzling and Estella's a woman and it makes her heels taut and real. He's warm and smells of some sweetness and he says I drove at 80 all the way down the motorway to get here quicker. I drove straight here to see you, he says, and, oh, how I've missed you. And Estella's hair is yellowy blonde and there's a strength in her legs and a poise in her heels and he's hers and he's come back to her and he's missed her and he's sorry he had to go away and he hates being away from her and he loves her and he won't go away again. Just like a real city gent; this is how the commuters would be, in private. And there's a blending between them, a total obliteration of any space between their two bodies, and an utter, an immaculate consummation of Estella and Estella's body. Because of his. And when they unfurl and it's time for wine and digestives she thinks there's no-one in the world who will ever love her this way: make such loving inside her: fill spaces and spaces inside her with yellow sunlight and warmth and the taste of wine and the feel of it, in her whole body. So she smiles, and she says, I hope she got off all right. With no problems. To test him out. And there's a faint cloud: a little overcast bit between the sunlight in her and the sunlight outside the window. It puts his face in shadow. Estella wishes he didn't take it so hard. She'll get by without him there above the sunlight, in a sky above their sky. Above the clouds, flying in the Jumbo, to another land. And he says, oh, by the way, I have to be in later, in case the phone rings. And there's a little shock; a little wrench, in the centre of Estella's body. And a voice says It's got to stop. It's got to stop. Estella repeats the phrase inside her head, silently, making a space for anger, to set in the space between them. To make him see. To push and thrust at him. Willing a change; striving with her whole body to cut the space, to slice it. To make him bleed.

They get in the car and they travel fast roads and they pass other cars with other couples in and they stop at a pub and they drink martinis. Well, Estella drinks martini; he drinks a pint of bitter. He gets it for her; he brings it to her; she sits at a table; she looks out on the sea wall; she watches the children play; keeps her eye on them. And then a group of bright and erotic and sparkly Jamaican people come dancing by. Walking fast on high stilettos; they wear pink and black and silver, jiggling their bare tanned shoulders, running, colourful, enviably distracting. And Estella sips her martini and feels it sparkle inside and she's with them too. It will be like this. Thinks Estella. This is what it will be like. But it's like it already; so what's the cutting edge, the little space of abrasion, inside? What's the shimmer, the glimmer of a wrench? She sees, in her mind's eye, a couple, walking together in this very place. This same space. They laugh, or smile, or pass remarks, and there's a big backdrop of space with no anxiety in. A whole large part of it that they can take for granted. A whole large sheet of it that they don't have to notice. They can be seated, outside the pub, at a table by the sea wall, watching their children; making sure they're safe. Or they can dance off to the disco with the pink and silver ones. Either of the spaces: it's interchangeable – but always in the same blank space of ease, that Estella will always, she knows, look out on. Something out there she will never penetrate. And the couple, the man and the woman, who signify the capacity for that special kind of ease, are the black haired woman and he. In a world Estella will never enter. Because she knows the system too well. Why doesn't he know? He says, shall we go and get Jonathan? Hey, let's go and get Jonathan. I bet he could do with a pint. Because he saw the couple too. And for him it's a sin and a crime against the only system he knows, to be an outsider.

She's running up the stairs, on the soft white carpet, in her thin, high heels. Running up flight after flight and for a moment quite alone in a space that holds promises. Up and up to where he lives at the top of the house and, as she goes higher, becoming more elated. Light on her feet, with the white wine light in her body. And now Jonathan shares the same space with his smile, and truly is happy. Because he's there for her. And, watching her, loves the sparkle in her eyes; the shimmer in her body. And likes it all the more, knowing that in a special way he can be the one who's closest to her, because he knows more about the way spaces arrange themselves. Sees her in cubism; knows that she'll turn and turn again and still there'll be other faces to her. And, knowing her thus, already, smiles a smile that takes her in, and of course wants a drive and a drink, to watch her burst alive and scatter little sprinklets of smiles and excitement. Wants to be there to see. To walk in her wake. And down they go. She sits in the front of the car and trails her whole naked arm along the back of her seat, drawing him in. Loving him for knowing about the blanks, between spaces. Drawing him in, though there's nowhere in he can go. And they drink and they laugh and later they speed in the dark and go to get hamburgers and she tastes all three. All the time touching, touching, reaching for the man. Trailing her foot against his leg; brushing his neck with her fingertips. Willing him to think ahead, to make a new space for her. Hating the borrowed spaces, the cheating, hating the loving him? No, laying proud claim to the loving him. But seeing, always, a silver thread of it, broken. Tinsel, after Christmas, just one stray strand of it. Too small to be worth keeping. Or the thread of a spider's web, broken and trailing into nowhere. Tapering off, so fine you'd hardly notice it. Unless you knew it was there.

And they take Jonathan home and they go on driving and he must come into her room in the dancer's house (at this hour, the dancer is sleeping) and love her into a space where there is no other dark-haired woman. She hears his feet crunch on the gravel. She hears the car door slam. She even hears the engine start, and it's just like in the movies, except that she can't see her own beautiful face, softly vivid with tears. She can't see her elegant and sad body, draped. She doesn't light a cigarette and smooth her hair. She leaps; she runs, there are shocks and wrenches running through her body. She pulls on some clothes, and her whole body is moving too fast and too desperate. She runs out into the night. It's important how fast she goes. She must go as fast as possible, to stretch her body to its limit. If there is any energy left in her body, it will remain, taut in her legs, torturing her, making her scream, causing the world to spin, the light to be too bright. And so she runs to the park, into the pit of black, where there's danger. She runs until she's cold and her heart's beating and she's crying with the small fragment of energy still left in the pit of her, which won't go away. And as she runs she begins, gradually, to move more slowly. Into the world where people and babies and lovers in stories are sleeping. She begins to see, as she gets colder in the night air and it's harder to keep on running, that everyone is asleep, in the real world, and in the story books. And now even he is asleep, and it will soon be tomorrow and time to start again. And back in the room it's bright and it's messy and her bed's the only space in the world where there can be peace and she nestles down and softly sleeps, and it is all obliterated.

*   *   *

The next day Estella went shopping. She could get a big plastic carrier bag and fill it until it was round and white. She bought gruyère and cheddar and some emmental and some jarlsberg, big tubs (not little) of coleslaw, some bars of chocolate, lots of salad and fruit, some wine, some cream, some more coffee and another packet of digestives. She liked the deli counter and the chocolate counter because both of those tastes were rich and indulgent. It all cost her ten pounds. Or thereabouts. And what was most exciting was that all the other women were there, all doing it. There were young blondey ones pushing prams with babies in and children straggling alongside. There were glamorous ones in tight white trousers and hair from the hairdresser's and perhaps dark glasses. There were older ones in Bally shoes and peachy pink nails and a look of having been doing this all these years. There were glamorous ones who stepped out of Sprites and ones in long traily dull dresses and green tights. There were all varieties and all colours and all ages and all styles of women, and, there at the shops, they were all together, juxtaposed. And Estella was there with them. She was doing it too.

* * *

Eating cheese and coleslaw and deli salami all the afternoon to the heat and the music. Tasting all the different tastes and eating all the coleslaw in the tub, now all at once. Starting to throw the pots and the packages away. Starting, already and with relief, to forget it all. Working towards an empty fridge, sitting on the floor in the filtered sun. Expanding and expanding in the bright heat, and sinking, heavier and heavier, nearer the ground. The book at her side. No-one in the house. Empty packets and pots rising in the little basket under the table. Getting so tired of it that even when he arrives, running, always running, she is weary of him. When he gets here he does nothing with his mind or his body for a full few minutes, except make tea; pour tea; drink tea, so that Estella's asking, with the voice inside her, Where are you? Even then when he's, at long last, in the room, under this roof, Estella's getting so tired of it that she can only remain on the floor. Negating the space that creates Estella. Denying herself. Fading out. Phasing out. And he's gone, this time, and he didn't eat the salami and he didn't love her he just strode and strutted and talked in a space of his own and Estella's intolerably heavy and there is nowhere for her to be and so she stays in the room but so bright is the light and so vivid and surreal the furniture that unless you looked quite closely, there in the foreground, you would hardly know she was there.

*   *   *

Yes, it's him. Estella, kneeling on the floor in the dust, ear to the phone, hears his voice in the room. The glow is back in her body. She's running down the street, she's running to meet him. She'll turn the corner and he'll be there. It's bank holiday, a day for convention, a day for outings. A day real people allow themselves and oh, mercy, the dark-haired woman is over the seas and safely far away. No bank holiday for her, ha ha. And Estella's happy and running, and she feels as natural and as right and as real as the sunlight itself. And walks as far as the park and sits on a bench to wait for him. What will they do together? Perhaps they will kiss under the trees, or walk hand in hand along the seashore, like a real couple. And his silence and his warm breath are there behind her and he's here. But there's a space between. A cloud. The cloud is Estella's boredom, and the missing link, massed between them. They walk hand in hand, they walk for a long way. Soon be there, he says. Where. Thinks Estella. What for. Why are you doing this. They walk to the sea. They sit on the cobbles. Punks in shiny coloured trousers balance on a wall on the cobbles and fight and scrap like cats or small children. He watches them as though just to watch were to pass comment and to pass comment suggested knowledge, and it was his special knowledge that characterised him, and that she would admire.

Before you came here, he said, when you knew you were coming and thought about what it would be like to be here, did you want to live by the sea? No, said Estella. I did, he said. In one of those houses over there, with the sea just across the road. To wake up in the morning, and open the window and look out on the sea. It is rhetorical. As though it's his poem, or something. Estella loves her faded, crumbling house in the dusty street, the dancer's house. There is nowhere she would less have liked to live, than facing the sea. I like the city, she said. I like privet hedges with dusty leaves, and commuters walking to the station. I like office clothes and I like houses with delicate, spindly furniture and sombre paintings. Like your dancer's house, he says. Not seeing why, at all. But to see the sea, he says. To open the window and see the sea and hear the seagulls. I suppose it would be nice in the Summer, says Estella. Thinking of the holiday-makers: commuters with less clothes on. They get up, then, and walk, and have an ice-cream, and walk again. It is cooler than it looked. Estella never wanted to live by the sea. She wanted to live in a big house with a heavy gate: a heavy pair of gates. But gates onto the road. So that when people passed and decided they'd look in, they would pull the heavy chain that rang a bell, and Estella would come out in her black dress and admit them. Pip stood before her. What? She looked again and Pip was standing before her in the road, staring up at her quite blankly. Looking from Estella to the man. He had a small rubber bucket in his hand, full of pebbles. Hello, he said. The man looked away. Hello, said Estella. She said, You made me jump; what are you doing here? Pip said nothing. Estella's heart was beating too fast for nothing. He'd given her a start. Jolted her out of the borders of this day; thrust her back into its futile centre. Pip just looked. You're very brown, said Estella. I hardly recognised you. Your face is pink, said Pip. Why is it pink? Don't you go brown in the sun? Estella said, Some people's skin is very fair and that makes it vulnerable in the sun, and then it goes pink before it goes brown. It means their skin is more delicate. And better, she said. Pale skin is more beautiful, for a woman, she said. And he was silent. The man smiled. We have to go now, said Estella. I hope you find lots more pebbles. Pip stared. Estella skirted round him and the man followed. When Estella looked back Pip was walking slowly in the other direction, slowly, and studiedly.

How can they be so serious? says Estella to the man. Why are children so absorbed? Why does whatever they're doing matter so much? Why are they so lucky? Oh, I dunno about that, says the man, because this is too real a question. Children are to be saved for the other world. The world of absolutes, the world of planning and certainty. And he doesn't want such realism in the haunted world he inhabits with Estella. This, at least, Estella deduces. The man is blank. The man looks on, benevolently, passively, into some middle distance. The cheating purgatorio. Where the end will present itself like a sheer drop. Unconnected with its beginning. Superimposed. And Estella goes on, relentlessly, urging some connection. Why are they so stubborn? She says. Why are they so – immovable; so – intractable. Because they only have one version of reason. He says, conceding to help her out. They only have one way of working things out; so they just carry on. They just stick at it, and you know that whatever happens things will work themselves out; they don't have to make any choices. So they can concentrate better. He says. Concentrating; joining in; thinking up an answer. I wouldn't have any patience with mine. Says Estella. I'd hit them if they screamed. I'd hit them and shout at them. She walks straight; walks tall. She practises her dancing in the morning, and it gives her a smooth, straight spine. No you wouldn't, he says. Of course you wouldn't. He runs with her under a tree, as a kind of joke (hiding from the world, having a secret) and kisses her, and Estella feels she's standing on warm earth, and the tree is verdant and growing, and that soon he'll just walk out of it all; step smartly over the horizon. And cries to him in her heart to regret it soon enough to stay. And knows that this would be the wrong order; for him, an impossible order.

They walk back up the tree lined street together and she

wonders what there can possibly have been in this day, with her, for him. An antidote to loneliness. She was a bucket of pebbles. Something to concentrate on, when the others (the other) were too busy for him. She was a bucket of pebbles. Her body was a bucket of pebbles. They walk together up the crumbling steps. And he says, Now I can't stay long, mind. Go to hell, say the pebbles. Get lost, says a big boulder in the centre of Estella's body. So in they go, and she lazes on the bed and he makes jasmine tea in a Japanese pot. And it's time for him to go. Alas. What a lovely sunny day it has been. And the door shuts and he's gone. This is a dream. Says Estella, and she says it out loud. This is a fiction. And she cries because she obeys and she complies and in her heart she makes plans, and all the time he's there at her side without being there. There and nowhere. Oblique, like the shape his smile makes. Intangible; a few words on a page, without a story. Not even that. A blankness, impossible to make sense of.

* * *

O.K. says Estella. All right, then, I will be alone. I will walk the streets alone and I will be so colourful that everyone will notice me and someone will want me. I will be substantial. I will have a brightly coloured body, bright as a body in a painting. I will live and breathe my own image; I will transport my own reflection, and transfix the gazes of others in its gaze. And there in the wardrobe Estella smells the faint fragrance, musty and perfumed, of Estella. She caresses the shoulders of each garment, thin slivers and blades of dull black. Taffeta; silk; velours and smooth velvet; mohair and angora for soothing. And selects. Pick a garment, any garment. Estella's playing now. If Pip was there, he'd play too. Estella looks over her shoulder: he's not there. And Estella flicks her fingers along the row and flips a garment, pulls it off the rail with a flourish, like a tailor.

Estella whisks the flat body of the dress off the rail, swirls it onto the bed, to wait. And undresses, without even a glance at her own body, waiting only to see it draped black, take shape. It's a pleated skirt. Flat, concertina pleats, cool, unyielding (provocative) to the touch, a hard, a glossy (a tarty) finish. Estella swirls, in the skirt, and makes a flat surface in the air around her, a circle to cut the air. A knife edge; a cutting blade; her body the pivot, she's rising up out of it, the plastic ballerina in the musical box. But black. She pulls on a tight black leotard: up, under the skirt, up over her torso, taut, like a dancer. Stretches it over her. And she's black as a slice of night; red. Streaked red, with scarlet stockings. Streaked red with grease paint; red with the brothel; red with the blood of the knife. Too much. Too much, Estella. Don't overdo it. After all it's only play. Only pebble-collecting. So Estella runs into the dancer's room and peeps behind the door; looks into the tarnished mirror. There's a blotchy, dappled image of Estella. Streaked with red; too bright. And so she runs back and she peels and slides threads of silk and there are black and red streaks of fraying fabric and faded taffeta in the air and Estella has black stockings. Estella has her small mirror, propped up over the sink, one of her own, just for her face. She sees a little, pretty face, a calm, a bored face, a face from somewhere else. Hard and cold. And seeing that coldness she pulls off the pleats, which concertina to the ground in a flourish. In a heap of pleats at her feet. And she steps out, with high steps, and into another skirt. A faded, dark deep blue skirt, a midnight skirt, one she bought in a theatre bar, because the actress had worn it, in the play. So warm and so Estella, though, that it lacks the cutting edge she needs to chisel a new Estella, for the night. To make a new image; a plastic one. Just for tonight. Aha, says Estella, and she's a pierrot, and marionette, in a one piece outfit with harem trousers. The legs of it are so circular and so billowy, the ankles tight, that it makes her want to dance. She's light on her feet, dancing tap; without the sound.

And then she heard the phone ringing.

Part Nine

Tears streaming hot on her face, Estella runs back into the room; this room, which, shockingly, has with a dull wrench become a different room: somebody else's room or a room in a nightmare. Has pulled itself out of the setting that had given Estella's body its reality. And thrown all the traces away; and washed them up.

And so running, at seven in the morning, she finds even the road has changed. Can it be brighter? It is still brighter. Bright with vermilion leaves and the silver grey slate of roofs. Bright with colouring book colours that must mean, that have to mean, that Estella's body is sick. For what body in its right mind would create colours so vivid, so early in the morning, so soon after the night, just by running, and by still running, and not stopping. It feels like the same day as the day Estella arrived in the street with her suitcase full of bright underwear for the theatre. The very same day, with all the spotlights on; the same set. There is no time between that day, and this dazzling moment. Estella feels again, the same smell of grease-paint. Choking her throat. Tears, fierce in her voice. Running, so fast her legs must give way. They must buckle under her body and Estella's body will be face down on the grey, the slate, the slices of pavement. Though not Estella's face any more because crushed and smashed and trodden underfoot by the commuters, filing up the street, over the remains of Estella.

What was this strange sunlight? Could it really be true? Could it really show, thus, in the world? It showed in the world: it showed banana yellow. But it didn't show in the people; they were coloured drab and pale. They looked: they looked before them and at their newspapers and up the road for their buses. But they didn't look changed by the strange yellow of the sunlight. They did look at Estella, though. She was crying on the bus at 7.30 in the morning. She cried to break. Her body splintered. How could she not break down, breaking thus. Shimmer shimmer, went the world; her tears shone. Real things rocked. Estella lost, on the bus at 7.30 that day, the sense that she was real among the things in the world. Her body was out of it all, and just not stable enough; though just, also, much too vivid.

In a café, carpeted, for comfort, clean and quiet, for comfort, Mercy waits. The other side of the table. On it, two milky coffees. Estella asks Mercy, why does my body feel like this. And Mercy is so soft as she smiles just slightly, that it's as though Estella were the little baby Mercy. Mercy smiles a little for Estella's sake, through sad eyes, and explains. Your body is your medium. When your body feels shock it's assuring you of your own autonomy. Your body focuses itself on the other people it needs. When one of the people is removed, your body has nowhere to focus any more. And Estella cries with relief that it's supposed to happen this way, and somehow that's a consolation. The man has gone. He left, as Estella had tried to know he would. How long will it take, asks Estella, what will happen? It's a false comfort, this café, warm with a milkiness, the warmth of human nourishment, so early in the morning. Estella had looked into the room and seen the dancer. Her feet were bare, painted scarlet. It made her feel the day distorted. Because this is one of those days that are wrenched out of real time: hospital days; going abroad days. Shock days. Not real days. Time out of mind. Days that ignore the body's time scheme. The café is a false comfort. Mercy's face is painted all over in a scarlet mask. Here is the light, brilliant through the window, casting a strong yellow light into the room, and bathing the face of Estella. Estella cannot adjust to the banana yellow light; the room will not settle itself.

What would happen, if nobody found out? How would they recognise it, anyway, even if they saw what had happened?

Absurdly, startlingly, with shocks, like electric shocks, through her chest and her legs, Estella could not feel herself, in the room. Her body, or the room, was dizzying, and prickling. Wizzing. Dazzling. So fast, in such lurching feelings of stabbing and dizzying, that she seemed to be moving, though she knew, from looking in the mirror, that she was actually standing still. She could not seem to feel that she, Estella, was really there in the room, any more. Estella looked in the mirror and she looked there with a feeling of being hurled and flung, and of not knowing what to want to see.

To see her own face, a little pale, greyish, and drawn. Even to see this face, might not be real. Because of the memories, images, imprinted on the mind, of faces you come to know, as, for Estella, Estella. Estella forces herself. But whether you can see that effort, that muscle in the stomach as she lifts it, poised, whether there is anything to see, though there is a big wrench in the pit of Estella, big enough to pull out everything that, for Estella, is Estella, whether there is any image of this, anything you can capture and see with your eyes and your mind, whether there is, and there isn't anything else in the sentence. And that is what Estella's mind is doing. This is how it's circling: all dead ends. Unfinished; the mind, it seems, falling apart, like the wedding dress. And where has the rest of it gone? No signs of it left behind. The nymphs are departed . . .

No cigarette ends, where she usually found them, in the morning, on the top of the brown table by the side of her bed; stubbed out and squashed on a little blue saucer. From the small yellow cupboard. No wine bottle, though she goes round the dazzling room, searching. Searching on purpose, to make sure, to test out what it felt like to search: to know what you were looking for, to look for a thing, an object, in a room, and pick it up and throw it away. Trying to stabilize the mind. There might have been a coin, dropped from the trouser pocket, and so Estella crouches down and looks, under the bed. There have been, in the past, these objects. A coffee cup, with a stain of coffee in a crescent in the bottom. But there they were, the cups and the saucers, leaning and drying on the draining board. And she knew there would be nothing. She wanted to be sure there had to be nothing, the actual indisputable fact that now, in this case, there was actually nothing, that nothing remained, was a thing she had to be sure of. And this was good, because it gave her something to do which had measurable results at the end of it. But it didn't quite work, because she knew already. Because, running, even then, in the same way, at the same speed, after running down the road, bright with the street lamps, masking the dark, pushing, thrusting her whole body into it, at once weightless and immovably heavy, after turning her whole body into the world after him, she had run back again, up the hill, turning back as a way of making it impossible to catch him up, impossible to be with him, when it was the end. Yet she must still make it impossible to feel the end; to feel her own body, Estella, at the end IT IS NOT THE END IT IS NOT IT IS NOT IT IS NOT there were hot tears on her face and someone would surely, must surely, see what had happened and be able to help her. Because he would leave her to break. Impossible, though, to find a way out of it, because how could he leave her, broken, when if she was broken like this she would never be the same any more so that what he left behind was not Estella. If she were to die or go mad there would be an explanation; but she would not die and she would not go mad.

It was the night: Estella broke free of her dreams with a wrench and searched the room, thus, for cigarette ends. When she found none, she went back to her bed and, pulling the pillow length-ways down beside her and squeezing it hard, she tried, again, to sleep.

* * *

The phone is ringing and ringing, ruthlessly, in the lurching, dazzling, very bright morning. Two terrible things have happened. Both mean the world of the dancer's house is destroyed. Both deny its ever having existed. One belongs to the night before; the other belongs to the morning. Estella's body is wrenched. It is thin strings, pulled this way and that between the two. The sunlight dazzles her eyes, and the world, or her body, is shaking. In amongst the shaking and the splintering of the light: fear, and guilt. It shakes with nothing: everything shattered, and with the holding on so tight and so hard and so desperately, to Estella, who is disintegrating in the splinters. Her body fizzles like the last light in an old bulb.

She tries and tries to train her mind along a line of some dull logic, any vague, dull line of it. Forces it along the tightrope, the knife-blade. Urges it away from the splintering light, towards some deeper darkness. She must pull all this together inside her, for Mercy's sake.

Estella is guilty, and as such she is fettered, tethered. This is bondage. Like standing behind two high, black wrought iron gates which were opened only by drawing heavy bolts across: swinging chains. And were closed irrevocably. Only the hangman with the mask could open them. The bolts were drawn, against Estella. The chains were fixed in place. Estella had no keys, and, in any case, she was observed. Any attempts on her part to escape would be thwarted. Though long ago, it had been her job to open the gates. To admit visitors. She is in the café, draped with its gingham table cloth, in the warm room, to the smell of cakes and toast. In the banana yellow light. She must stop it getting in. Mercy is seated on the other side of the table, untinted, her face drawn, drained of colour, the face of the women who fade themselves out, the better to turn the spotlight on other people's needs.

It was Estella's fault. There was still, there must be still, a Mercy more wreathed and bright and tinted than all the firebirds in Arabia – and that Mercy was still here at the table. But the layers had got reversed. Now, the colour was underneath, and the pale, naked skin, the canvas for painting, was on the surface. That must be the explanation for the change. But, meanwhile, Mercy was here pinched and drained and nowhere in any of the surface spaces of the persistent yellow light, mastered by loss.

It couldn't be Mercy's fault, this absence of Mercy. It must be Estella's. Because Mercy was thus changed and Estella was not. Except for the spiders in the pit of her stomach. Blaming her, blaming her. And the light dazzling, and her body falling apart. It was Estella's fault because she had used the dancer's house, with Mercy and the baby Mercy secreted in the very basement and subterranean pit of it, to play. And only babies played. It had been the baby Mercy's right to take the stage, in play. Estella should have looked on, as she worked. Should have been content to watch. Because it was right to be in the wings. She had known this, but she should have trusted it. Should not have wanted to test it out. To claim the stage for her own small rehearsals. It was the baby's turn. Estella should have passed by the basement every morning with her portfolio and her newspaper, wearing a smooth skirt and heels somewhere in the no-man's land between high and low. And waved to the baby, on her way to the train, to get busy.

Or she could have lived in the underworld, like Mercy, in the basement half-light where women stood about in the shops at eleven in the morning in old stilettos and only half their make-up. But only if she had a reason. Babies whose clothes had to be washed, babies who screamed and stuck jam, or school children with recorders who stared at your big body and thought it felt like theirs, only bigger. And you could not explain that it did not. Could not tell them about its shadows and its curtains and the way it divorced itself from you, and the pain of it. She could have done all that. But not on her own, without the staring, and the washing. This world alone was a dangerous world. Things would pass you by in it. You started further back in the line of commuters. You could not get to the front, you had to stand, in the train. It was like that forever, if you had been in the underworld, in the basement where the children played. Beautiful women with hair like meringue and no chips in their nail varnish had got ahead. Even the masked women, masks superimposed on drained and drawn canvas of skin which somehow showed in the mask. Their hips too broad. Their casseroles in the oven. Even these would get in front.

There was no space for desire in the underworld. This is what Estella had learned. It looked, from above, as though down there in the shadows desire found its colours, its taffetas and its stilettos, and no work thwarted it and chained it and kept it at bay and in order. But it was not so. It was not so. Mercy had no place to be, now, and her face, drained of colour, was somehow not in the room. Even in the no-man's land of the café. For the baby had died in the night.

* * *

But what could Estella do, for Mercy. How could she help her. What piece of her could she let go, for Mercy's sake. It seemed she could never assuage the weariness of Mercy, a weariness which would now last for ever, making a mask of her old brightness, casting a shadow between it and her tired face. In the night the baby Mercy had been sleeping softly. In the morning she did not wake up. They did not know what happens to the baby in the cot, when this happens. It is no-one's fault. Returning to the world from this loss Mercy was still away somewhere. She could not come back to life. Estella wished for a papa with black patent shoes to take Mercy against his stiff black suit and cradle her head on his shoulder. She wished for a French papa with an Alfa Romeo, who would soothe Mercy with sheer speed. The world was too slow for this loss, and the light too banana bright.

Estella takes Mercy's hand and cannot help her, and tries and tries to soothe her with her own thoughts, but they will not settle in any space that can comfort Mercy. There is so much to understand, a whole network, in layers, of it, and yet nothing. It seemed the baby Mercy had been a part of the woman and now the little playing part had gone, Mercy would never feel pleasure again. It seemed, after all, that it was the baby Mercy who had breathed a tinted and garish magenta glow into the body of the mother. The part that strode and leaned on bars, scarlet, and was real, not pretending or rehearsing. The part of Mercy's brightness that made her paint real. There was the wreathed and painted, the tinted and magenta-glowing Mercy. And there was the pale, drained canvas of her. And there had been something between them, folding them together. What had been between them, was the baby.

Mercy has to go away. In the basement, in the subterranean world, the spaces have hard edges now. Mercy will go somewhere where she can skim the surface. Where the shadows will not brush against her like knife blades. They go out together into the unremitting light. Estella says, I can't believe it happened without its being somebody's fault. Mercy does not talk. She shakes her head softly. But then her face breaks into splinters.

In the banana yellow light, threading among the crowds of people, Estella's body feels more her own than it has ever felt. But she cannot reach it. In the banana yellow light, is Estella's body. In the banana light, is Estella. And there is something between them. But what is between them, splinters in the light.

Part Ten

It's dim but bright in the early morning, the light filters weakly through the mist. Estella leaves the dancer's house early, to catch the train. She said goodbye to the dancer the night before. Is that packet of Persil empty, asked the dancer. Do you want me to throw it away? So, it was not a sentimental parting. I'll be back, said Estella, I'll come back to see you. Yes, yes do come back, the dancer said. Do come back. And she smiled up at Estella, from the dusty room, as though she knew this was an ending, the last of this particular Estella.

And so in the early, misty morning Estella leaves alone. She looks back at the dancer's house and sees: it still holds its promises. But the real secret is, that no-one will fathom them. They belong to the house, just as its own secrets belong to the wedding dress. And so Estella makes her way down the street, too early even for the commuters. Only a slight movement of the air causes her to look behind her. Pip has come out early to watch her go, and follows her down the road a little way. She takes his hand, and kisses the small forehead. Then she must go. As she rounds the corner, the small Pip still watches her, until she disappears. His forehead feels warm. She is sure to come back, one warm, bright day when he will have changed, grown up, and she will have stayed the same. Pip waits at the gate, for the day to come, and the image of pale and beautiful Estella, turning the corner in the distance, in the mist, will never leave him.

Part Eleven

On the station, along the platform, lined with dusty tracks, there is one train which gleams a pale blue-grey. Estella is walking along the platform. This is Paris, and the air has changed. This dust is the dust of gauloises and a faint thread of perfume, and, faintly, garlic. Now it is the end of the Autumn and space is closing in for the coming dark nights. Estella is tensed in her diminishing space, and carries her folder and a suitcase. Her change is loose in the pocket of her skirt. In her stomach, a thin ledge, on which the things she sees as she looks about her settle themselves among the things already there. Estella is on her way, to a life where work fits, and the design is taut and tightly woven, already. All the pieces of it fit together, and Estella will be slotted in. She will feel important, and soon she will be noticed, and people will know who she is.

The station is grey dust. On the platform beside her Estella notices a faded green machine for minuscule pieces of chewing gum. Chewing gum is smaller in Paris. It takes up only a thin, thin thread of the world, and it keeps its edgy, reedy flavour. In England the chewing gum is bigger and brighter. There are too many wrappings on it. It is too pink. It soon tastes of yourself. In England even the chewing gum gets you involved. Estella stands back, already. The glorious autonomy of Parisian life. She walks at one remove, already, from the day, along the platform. As she walks she looks up at the train. From one of the windows, she sees two hands, the nails painted scarlet, resting on the window ledge. The fingers balance a gauloise, the smoke is flicked; falls. Estella walks towards this carriage. She steps the high step up into the train, and pulls her suitcase and her folder up behind her.

In the carriage the French woman sits. Her feet rest on a small case. Her shoes are pale blue-grey kid. Her blonde hair is heaped and piled in furls and folds, like meringue. Her face all shaded apricot, and there is a measured translucence about her cheekbones. A fine ledge of bone, with shading all thinly powdered round it. She rests her arms along the window ledge. Opposite her, le mari is seated. His hair is very black and he reads a newspaper. His clothes look as though they would crackle. Estella goes to her seat. She props her folder up against it. She lifts her suitcase up onto the rack. As she sits down she notices that the Frenchman's shoes are highly polished; black, with laces: they dazzle and gleam. The French woman looks through to the other side of the glass. Estella begins her journey; settles herself to watch.

About the Author

Sue Roe, who is 25 and was born in Leicester, divides her time between writing, painting, and working as a publisher's editor responsible for an English literature list. She is also a freelance reviewer and is now working on her next book, a critical study. She took a first in English at the University of Kent and an M.A. at Sussex. *Estella: Her Expectations* is her first novel.